Low Tide:

Low Tide:

Prequel to the Caines Island Stories

Sherry Comstock

Sherry Comstock

First Printing, 2024

To my husband, Keith, who from the beginning said that I needed to tell Callie and Joe's early story.
To my children and grandchildren, you keep me feeling young enough to keep trying new things.

ACKNOWLEDGEMENTS

Authors have such a large supporting cast and I am no exception. My family always has wonderful words of encouragement. Words which keep me writing and lead me to delving into the internet to try and understand this writing business.

My critique group never seems to tire of Callie's story. Their support and honesty has been immeasurable on this writing journey.

My writing community with whom I trade information about all aspects of writing: as a craft and as a business. They have helped me grow as a writer.

My beta readers, Sarah Spear, Elizabeth Solazzo and Mary Turner, their diligence and thoughtful comments as they read my first draft were incredibly invaluable.

Finally, my readers, thank you for continuing to read my stories.

All these people and many more have my deepest gratitude and heartfelt thanks.

1

Caines Island 1969

Standing at the screen door in the living room, Callie watched the truck's taillights disappear behind the dense foliage of the live oak trees lining the road. Checking to see that her baby, Kimberly, was still asleep in her seagrass basket, she quietly opened the door and stepped out onto the porch. With her arms wrapped tightly under her breasts, she sank into a nearby wicker rocking chair. The December breeze carried a chill. Callie wrapped her arms tighter around herself and as she rocked slowly, she tried to take in everything Joe's boss had told her.

A large dump truck had slipped its gears and run into the wall and the scaffolding Joe was standing on. The collapsing wall trapped Joe beneath it. Although his fellow workers did everything they could, calling an ambulance and promptly digging through the rubble to free him. Joe died before it arrived. Fresh tears ran unchecked down Callie's cheeks. She knew there were things that she should be doing, like calling her parents and Joe's parents, but her grief-induced daze rooted her to the rocking chair. The melancholy sound of doves cooing broke up her thoughts.

Still in a daze, Callie went inside and was struck by the sight of the Christmas tree with its shiny ornaments and bright garland. *Just a few weeks ago we were opening presents and laughing. How can this be happening?* Checking on her daughter once more, Callie went into the kitchen. After taking several deep breaths, she called her parents.

"Hey, Momma, Joe was in—" Callie's voice broke as she struggled to keep from crying. With another deep breath, she managed to add "he was killed in an accident at work," before she began to cry again. Her mother let Callie cry for a little and then told Callie she and her father would leave when he got in from work. They'd be there after supper. Callie and her mother talked a little longer. "Thanks, Momma. I've got to call Joe's parents now," Callie said before hanging up.

Calling Joe's parents was harder. He was an only child. Then, too, his dad had a major heart attack several months ago. Melinda, Joe's mother, broke down completely while Callie told her about the accident. Melinda was so incoherent, Callie had to tell his dad everything to be sure they understood what had happened. *I hope this isn't too much for him.* She agreed to let them know when the details for the funeral service were final. *And how am I supposed to do that? I went to Aunt Sally's funeral, but her brother-in-law arranged everything. I don't know anything about arranging funerals.* Hearing Kimberly's cries, she got up to care for her infant.

2

Columbia 1964

Callie waited by the living room's large picture window and tried to peer around the edge of the curtains without the neighbors seeing her. Tonight was the Junior-Senior prom. Callie fidgeted with the bow sitting just under the bust of her empire waist formal. Her nervousness got the better of her, so she returned to her bedroom to check her appearance once more.

Staring at her reflection, Callie felt very grown up in her long gown and heels. Her pale blue dress had a darker, contrasting bow. Its color made her think of Texas bluebells she had seen in a picture once. The shoe store dyed her tiny kitten heels to match the bow. *This French twist makes me look so grown up. It sure is different from my ponytail.* Callie sighed as she turned and twisted, trying to look over her shoulder to see the back of her dress. She and Joe had been dating for two years. They didn't go to the prom last year. Neither one of them was sure of the other then. Smiling, she turned away from the mirror. *But now we know.*

"Callie, come here, sweetheart," her mother called from the living room.

Reminding herself to take smaller steps in her long dress and heels, she joined her mother. Lydia, her mother, waved an arm toward the electric fireplace Callie's dad had gotten her last Christmas. Although they had one of the larger homes in the community because her dad was a supervisor, mill houses didn't come with fireplaces and her mother had always wanted one.

"Stand by the fireplace. I want to get a picture of you before Joe gets here," her mother said.

"Yes, ma'am." Callie crossed the room. "Joe should be here any minute. I hope he remembered the color of my dress so the corsage matches."

"I'm sure he got it right," her dad said as he turned in his recliner to get a look at his daughter. "Callie-girl, you look extra beautiful tonight," he added with a smile.

Callie blushed and lowered her eyelashes a moment before her mother told her to smile and took the picture. Blinking to clear the colored lights caused by the brightness of the flashbulb, Callie's heart fluttered when she heard a vehicle pull into the driveway.

"Oh, I think that's Joe," she said as she started for the door.

Her mother stepped between Callie and the door. "Slow down. Let Dad get the door. Maybe you should go check your makeup?"

Callie hesitated; *I just did all that.* After she turned to go down the hall, she rolled her eyes in response to her mother's harsh tone. *It'll just be easier to do what she wants.*

Looking in the bathroom mirror, Callie heard the knock on the door. Unable to contain her excitement, she started back toward the living room. "Come on in, Joe," her dad said opening the door.

Suddenly tentative, she paused on the threshold between the hall and the living room and watched Joe walk into the house. *He's so good-looking.* "Ah, yes, here's Callie," her dad said as he caught sight of his daughter.

"Hey, Callie." Joe's voice croaked a little. Clearing his throat he continued. "Uh, this is for you." He held out a clear plastic container with tiny blue flowers inside. His dark brown nearly black curly hair made a close cap on his head, and his rented tuxedo fit well on his tall lanky frame.

Callie opened the container holding pale blue tea roses tipped with a darker shade of blue and smiled up at Joe, "They're beautiful. The blue is perfect." She fumbled a bit trying to get the roses out of the crinkly package.

"Here, let me help," Joe offered and took the package from Callie. "I got one for your wrist. The florist said a lot of young women like them."

He managed to get the corsage out of the package despite his shaking hands and placed it on Callie's outstretched arm. With the corsage in place, she held her wrist up in front of herself to better see the flowers. "They're lovely. Thank you." Joe took Callie's hand and turned toward the door.

"Not quite so fast," her mother spoke up. "I want a couple more pictures, and I promised your mother I would give her some, too Joe."

Laughing, the two young people turned around. "Back by the fireplace, Momma?" Callie asked.

Her mother nodded and orchestrated a few more poses before she and Callie's dad walked them onto the front porch.

"The dance is over at eleven, right?" Her dad asked.

Callie nodded and Joe said, "Yes, sir, Mr. Parsons."

"All right, I expect to see you back here at eleven-thirty," he said seriously. "Now go have a good time," he added with a smile.

In keeping with the theme, the Age of Aquarius, the prom committee had suspended constellations representing the twelve houses of the zodiac from the gym ceiling. They had the requisite punch and other snacks along with napkins printed with a picture of the zodiac and "class of 1969". A DJ played songs like "Sugar, Sugar" and "Grazing in the Grass". Callie and Joe danced to virtually all of them, but their song was "My Cherie Amour" by Stevie Wonder. Callie thought it utterly romantic as Joe whispered the lyrics in her ear as they danced.

When they returned from the dance, the porch light was on. Joe took the keys from the truck's ignition. As he leaned toward Callie to kiss her, she moved away. "Let's go up on the porch. I'll never hear the end of it if you don't walk me to the door," she said, moving toward the truck's passenger door.

The porch swing creaked when Callie and Joe sat down, and her dad stuck his head out of the front door. "Don't be too long out here," he said.

"Yes, Dad. I'll be in soon," Callie answered. Her father closed the door. "See, I told you," she giggled and leaned closer to Joe.

Joe reached out to hold her hand. "After graduation, I'll be able to work full-time at the mill," he said while reaching into his jacket pocket. "I know you have another year of school, and your parents won't let you wear an engagement ring now." He hesitated. "But I bought you this little ring. Will you wear it? Then after you've graduated, and I've saved enough for a real engagement ring..." His voice trailed off.

Callie hugged Joe and kissed him, "Yes," she said, leaning away and slipping the ring on her finger. "This is beautiful. But my dad's going to be coming back out any minute. I should go in."

"I know you're right. Just one more hug and kiss before I go?" Joe held her close for a moment and then kissed her gently before standing up. "I'll call you tomorrow," he said, skipping down the steps.

Callie and Joe continued to date through her senior year of high school. With money she saved from babysitting and working in the mill during the summer, she began putting things away in the cedar hope chest her dad made for her last year.

Since Joe worked full-time at the mill and Callie was still in school, they only went out on a Friday or Saturday. But they were often at each other's homes for supper during the week.

Friday while studying at the kitchen table, she heard her father answer the phone. "Yes, Callie's here. Let me get her."

Hearing that the call was for her, Callie went into the living room. "It's Joe," her dad said, laying the receiver down and returning to his recliner.

"Thanks, Dad," Callie said, before sitting in the chair beside the small table that held the phone.

"Hi, Joe," she said into the receiver. She listened a minute before saying, "Let me ask. My Aunt Sally is coming for supper tonight."

She put the receiver on the table before returning to the kitchen. "Momma, is it okay if Joe comes to supper? He picked up an extra shift tomorrow, so we won't be able to go out later tonight like we planned," Callie looked earnestly at her mother. *I really don't want to wait until Sunday after church to see him.*

Callie's mother looked over her shoulder at her daughter. "Sure, sweetie. We'll eat about five. Tell him not to be late. Dad has to take your Aunt Sally home after supper. In fact, I think he just left to get her."

"Thanks, Momma," Callie said before hurrying back to the living room and picking up the phone. "Joe, are you still there?" She listened a moment before continuing. "Oh, good. Supper's at five, but come when you want. I've nearly finished my English paper."

Her dad had returned with Aunt Sally when Callie heard Joe's truck in the driveway. She really wanted to sit in the living room and talk with him, but knew her mother expected her help in the kitchen. Her dad winked at her over his paper when she hurried to open the front door.

Joe was nearly at the door when she stepped onto the porch. "Aunt Sally is already here, and I've got to help get supper ready," she said as she stood on tiptoe to give him a quick kiss before leading him inside.

"Would you like some iced tea?" she asked, closing the door behind them.

"Hello, Mr. Parsons," Joe said as he saw Callie's dad in the living room. He looked at Callie, grinning. "Sure, Callie. I'll come get it," he added and followed her into the kitchen.

Aunt Sally sat at the kitchen table folding napkins. She and Callie's mother stopped talking as the two young people came into the room.

"I'll just get Joe some iced tea and then I'll start peeling the potatoes, Momma," Callie said as she went to a cabinet to get a glass.

"That's fine," her mother answered. "We're right on schedule."

"Hello, Mrs. Parsons. Thanks for having me over for supper. And hello Miss Sally," Joe said as he paused in the kitchen doorway.

"It's good to see you, Joe," Callie's mom said. leaning against the counter.

"Glad we'll get a chance to visit," Aunt Sally said putting the stack of napkins in the center of the table. "It's been a while since I last saw you."

Callie gave Joe his tea and watched him return to the living room before she gathered everything and started peeling potatoes at the table. Listening to the talk drifting in from the other room, she was happy Joe liked sports nearly as much as her dad. Her mom liked him because he was respectful and never seemed to take Callie for granted. He graduated near the top of his class while holding down a part-time job his junior and senior year. Joe's dad and Callie's dad had worked in the mill together for years. Both families had the same set of basic values: work hard, family first and help others when you can.

"I'm sorry, what was that Aunt Sally?" Callie looked up at her aunt and smiled.

"I want to go to the island in a few weeks. Do you think Joe would drive me?" her aunt asked. "You could come with us."

"We can ask him. It might be a little tight in his truck if I go," Callie said and wondered what her aunt was up to.

"Well, I've still got my car, even though I don't drive anymore. We could take that," her aunt offered.

"It would be nice to see the island again. It's been so long since I've been there." Callie put the cut-up potatoes in a pot filled with water and her mother put them on the stove to boil. After wiping the table, Callie took plates from the cabinet so she could set the table.

"That's a long trip for a day, isn't it?" Callie's mother turned from the stove to look at her sister.

"Well, maybe it would be," Sally replied. "I don't think we can spend too much time on the island since the house is in such disrepair. I'd still like to find someone to do some repairs in the kitchen, and it would be good to see Alma, Max, and Louise, even for a little bit."

A hurricane damaged Sally's house on Caines Island a couple of years ago. While still living on the island and waiting for repairs to be made to the house, Callie's aunt had suffered a major stroke at thirty-six. Although her doctors had considered her recovery remarkable, Aunt Sally still had a slight limp and tended to tire easily. After her recovery from the stroke, Sally had purchased a house in Columbia, not far from Callie's parents.

As Callie brought the dishes to the table, Sally said. "If you just put things here, I'll set the table while you get drinks for everyone. I can walk along the table without my cane." Shrugging her shoulders Sally added, "I can't stand just watching people work while I sit and do nothing."

It wasn't long before Callie's mother mashed the potatoes and put hot biscuits on the table. She walked to the door leading into the living room and said, "Supper's ready."

Callie's dad sat at the head of the table with Callie's mother to his right. Aunt Sally sat next to her sister. Callie sat to the left of her dad, and Joe sat next to Callie.

As everyone began passing the dishes and serving themselves, Aunt Sally picked up the conversation she had begun with Callie and her mother. "Joe, would you be willing to drive Callie and me down to Caines Island next weekend?"

Joe looked around the table before answering, "Well, my truck---"

"I keep my car serviced. We could take that," Aunt Sally interrupted with a smile. "I need to make arrangements for some repairs, and I'd like to see a few old friends while I'm there," she continued while serving herself mashed potatoes and passing the bowl to Joe.

Joe served himself before passing the bowl to Callie. "I'm off the next couple of weekends. I have to make sure my parents don't need me, but yes ma'am, I could do that." Joe looked sideways at Callie and grinned.

Callie's mother, Lydia, frowned slightly, "Sally, are you thinking of going back to live on the island?"

"Oh no, Lydia. I wouldn't do that. I don't think I'll ever drive again after my stroke. We would have to start out early, but I think we could go there and come back in a day. What do you think, Joe? Does that seem reasonable for you?" Sally said before cutting her roast. "I'd just like to get the house in shape so I could spend a few days there, now and again."

"Yes, ma'am. We'd have to be on the road about six thirty or seven," Joe answered. He agreed to check with his parents, and the conversation turned to Joe's upcoming graduation in June. Joe reached out to hold Callie's hand, but let go when he saw her father watching.

Soon supper was over and Callie's dad drove Aunt Sally home. Joe hung around in the kitchen while Callie and her mother washed dishes. Afterward, her mother settled into an armchair, reading a magazine. The young couple sat close to each other on the couch in the living room talking quietly.

"Hey, Joe, Callie," her dad said, as he gave Callie's mother a kiss on the cheek before settling into his recliner and opening his copy of *Sports Illustrated*. "What time is your shift tomorrow, Joe?"

Joe sat up a little straighter and moved away from Callie on the couch. "I have to be there at seven. Oh, it's eight o'clock already," he said looking at his wristwatch. "I guess I should be going."

"I'll walk you to the door," Callie felt herself blush as she thought about the fact that the front door opened right into the living room. *Oh, man. How ridiculous was that?*

"Goodnight, Mr. and Mrs. Parsons, thank you again for having me over for supper," Joe said on his way to the door.

"Glad to have you here," her father said as they opened the front door.

"Callie, don't be out there long," her mother said as the young couple stepped onto the porch.

"Yes, ma'am," Callie answered before she closed the door.

On the porch, Joe pulled Callie close for a long hug and kiss. Callie backed away. "My parents are right in there. Let's not get carried away," she laughed softly. "You better go now, or I'll be grounded for sure."

Joe smiled. "I'll call you tomorrow when I get off," he said, walking down the steps. Callie watched him drive away before going inside.

3

Columbia/Caines Island 1964

Callie sat on the porch swing while she waited for Joe to pick her up before going to Aunt Sally's. She was excited to be returning to the island for the first time in a few years. A Carolina wren perched on the porch railing as it warbled its morning song before flitting off into a nearby stand of pine trees. Small fluffy clouds tinted pink by the early morning sun dotted the otherwise clear sky. It wasn't long before Joe's truck pulled into the driveway.

After a brief embrace, the young couple went inside to let Callie's parents know they were leaving. "Momma, Dad, Joe's here," Callie said, leading Joe into the kitchen where her parents were enjoying their morning coffee.

"Good morning, Mr. and Mrs. Parsons," Joe said as he trailed Callie into the kitchen. She gathered a few packages.

"Good morning, Joe," her father said. "It looks like a good day for a trip."

"Yes, sir. It does at that," Joe answered. Grinning, he watched Callie picking up Tupperware containers from the counter.

"Would you take a couple of these?" Callie asked and she turned to look at Joe. "I made some peanut butter cookies to take with us."

"Why so many?" He asked as he took the containers Callie held out to him.

"It's not as many as it seems," Callie said with a lopsided grin. "I just wanted to have a little something to give to Aunt Sally's friends on the island."

"Speaking of Aunt Sally." Her mother turned to look at the young couple. "You're going to be late if you don't get going."

Joe flicked his wrist to look at his watch, "You're right, ma'am. Callie, is there anything else you need?"

"Just my purse in the living room," she said. After giving each of her parents a hug, she added, "I'll grab it on my way out."

Aunt Sally lived a few blocks away, but not actually in the mill village. When she moved to Columbia a couple of years ago, she had planted a couple of redbud trees and a dogwood tree in her front yard. Even though their blossoms were long gone, their leaves provided some shade for the porch. Joe parked the truck in front of the house before helping Callie gather the cookies.

Aunt Sally stepped to the front door and locked it while the young couple walked up the driveway. Pointing to a large thermos and a picnic basket sitting on a nearby table, she said, "The car's unlocked. Callie, get a box from the storage room on the carport and then put your containers in it. Joe, would you get the picnic basket and thermos and put them in the trunk, along with the box?" After handing Joe her keys, Aunt Sally picked up her cane from the back of a chair and made her way carefully down the driveway.

Callie put the cookies in a box, gave it to Joe and was about to get in the backseat when her aunt called out, "Callie, you get in the front seat. I'll take the back." Joe waited to close the car door for Aunt Sally and slid behind the steering wheel. After taking a moment to look over the car's instrument panel, he backed slowly out of the driveway. The three travelers chatted for a while until Aunt Sally drifted off to sleep.

"Callie, do you have that atlas handy?" Joe asked a few hours later as they approached Charleston.

"Yeah, what do you need?" Callie asked. She pulled the atlas from under the seat and turned to the page for Charleston. Last night Joe had marked their trip with a ballpoint pen.

Before Joe could answer, Aunt Sally pulled herself to the edge of the backseat and said, "I'm awake now. I'll be able to help you get through Charleston and onto the island."

Callie turned in the seat to smile at her aunt. She was a short, slender woman. Her hair, once as dark as Callie's, now had wide bands of gray that spread from her temples. "I've missed coming to the island. We didn't go so much the last couple of years," Callie said.

"I know," her aunt replied. "The place grows on you, but there's a lot of repairs still to be made after that hurricane."

As they approached the bridge to Caines Island, Callie's excitement grew, and she moved closer to the window, peering out at the lush marshland. She remembered running on the beach and splashing along the water's foamy edge. Rolling down her window, she breathed deeply and stuck her hand out so it could bounce in the wind. "I love that smell---marshes, and salty air," Callie said and turned to look at Joe.

Joe grinned back at her. "Smells like bad fodder to me," he said with a wink.

Sally laughed and Callie playfully punched his shoulder. "How can you say that?" she asked as she moved closer to the window. "It's good old fresh air without any smoke from the mills in it." Callie leaned out the window, stretching to get a glimpse of the ocean.

Joe chuckled. "It sure is pretty." He slowed down as he drove onto the island's narrow road. Looking ahead, he asked, "Is this where we turn, Aunt Sally?" Vines partially obscured the street sign for Kiawah Trail.

Sally pulled against the front seat, leaning forward so she could see the road ahead. "Yes, that's it. My house is the third one on the left. Just after that empty lot on the corner."

Joe pulled into the driveway of the small white Cape Cod with black shutters. A screened-in porch stretched across the front and wrapped around to the left. Much of the screen was gone. The stump of a large tree remained in the yard.

"Aunt Sally, is that what's left of the tree that went through your roof?" Callie asked, pointing at the stump. "It's got to be at least three feet wide."

"Yes. It went through my bedroom. I was able to get the roof and the bedroom ceiling repaired pretty quickly. I'll have to see if I can get the stump taken out," she said shifting herself across the seat and preparing to get out of the car.

Callie hopped out as soon as the car stopped. Joe opened the door next to Sally and offered her a hand. "Let me help. Grab a hold of my arm. Maybe I can help with some of the repairs, especially once Callie and I are married."

Sally smiled at the young man's gallantry and took the offered arm. "Thank you, Joe. And we can talk more about what repairs need to be done later. Things are okay for a weekend visit, but I'd like it to be nice again," she said as she stood outside the car. Turning to pick up her purse and cane from inside the car she said, "I'll open the house; you and Callie get our things from the car."

"Yes, ma'am," Callie said while she tried to take in all the trees on the property. Several live oak trees played host to Spanish moss which fluttered in the breeze. There were redbud and dogwood trees, not to mention a large magnolia that had to be at least twenty years old. She even spotted a couple of peach trees.

They took everything except the suitcases into the kitchen. Callie and Aunt Sally began wiping down the counters and the kitchen table's white porcelain enameled top. Callie could see water stains along the walls and noticed the kitchen window needed replacing. Joe found a pair of gardening shears and went to remove the vines from the street sign. When Joe returned, Aunt Sally decided she was walking over to her next-door neighbor's. "Callie, why don't you two take a walk on the beach? The rest can wait until later," her aunt added. "We can eat when we get back."

The young couple walked along the shoreline, laughing at the antics of the brown and beige sandpipers dancing along the foaming water as it retreated to the ocean. After a while, they sat shoulder to shoulder simply watching the cresting waves make their way to shore. "We lived here for a while when I was little," Callie said digging her toes into the sand. "I've always missed it - the birds, the flowers, and everyone is so nice." Callie leaned her head on Joe's shoulder.

"We'll have to be sure to come back each year once we're married," Joe said. "Your Aunt Sally seems to miss it, too. Maybe we could bring her and stay at her place." His stomach growled loudly.

"That sounds like a good idea," Callie laughed. "But first, let's get you fed before you waste away to nothing."

Aunt Sally was setting lunch out in the kitchen when they returned, still laughing about Joe's stomach which kept complaining about the lack of food. Joe went to wash up in the bathroom and Callie went to the kitchen sink.

"Sounds like you guys had a good time," her aunt said. "I thought we'd go ahead and eat. Max should be home soon. Then we can visit for a while at Alma's. Do you remember him, Callie?" Sally put a plate of sandwiches and a bowl of potato salad in the middle of the table.

Callie turned from the kitchen sink where she stood washing her hands. "Yes, I remember Max. Big, tall Black man, close cropped hair. He's got the fishing boats." She frowned slightly. "And his wife is Louise, right? She's tall, too."

"You got it," her aunt smiled. "Anyway, after lunch, Alma asked us to stop by before going back to Columbia. Max and Louise will be there. I'd like you to meet them all." Sally sat down and motioned for them to join her when Joe returned from the bathroom.

"Sounds good, Aunt Sally," Callie said. After taking a few bites of her sandwich, she asked. "Did you get a hold of the repairmen?"

"Not everyone. But I did talk to someone about the stump. They'll take it out next week," Sally's brow creased, and she shrugged tilting her head towards her shoulder. "Not everyone is working today since it's Saturday, or at least they're not answering their phones."

When they finished lunch Joe put the picnic basket and thermos in the trunk of the car while Callie and her aunt straightened the kitchen. "Aunt Sally, I love your dishes," Callie looked at the turquoise blue plate before adding it to the other brightly colored plates in the cabinet.

"The pattern's called Fiesta," her aunt said. "The bright turquoise, yellow, and green colors just say 'beach' to me."

"Hmm, they do," Callie agreed and closed the cabinet door. She looked around the kitchen and dreamed of the day when she and Joe would have their own home.

Max and Louise were already at Alma's when the trio made their way across the yard. Callie smiled, watching Joe. Solicitous as always, he hovered beside Aunt Sally, ready with a steadying arm should she need it, but letting her make her own way whenever possible.

Everyone gathered on Alma's front porch for iced tea. Callie added her cookies to the spread on the table. She gave one box to Alma and another to Max and Louise. Louise had made cheese straws for the group as well. Her curly hair looked like a halo with the sun shining from behind. The big news was that Max was selling his fishing boats. His son, Steve, was in college and had definite plans to study law.

"You can't blame a young man for having his own dream," Max said smiling. "It'll give Louise and me a nice nest egg."

Sally smiled and nodded. "So, what will you do, Max? Never knew you to sit around."

"Well, we'll be able to put a little money back." Max shrugged. "People have started selling on the pier. Thinking about doing a little something there."

Louise smiled and rubbed her husband's shoulder. "I've still got the shop going. So we've got time for him to figure it out." Several years ago, Max built Louise a small salon on their property. She had several clients who traveled from neighboring towns for Louise to do their hair.

The sun moved closer to the western horizon. Aunt Sally stood up and stretched a little. "This has been wonderful, but I suppose we should get on the road. We don't want to be too late getting back to Columbia."

"Don't be so long next time," Alma said, her brown, nearly black eyes misting as she hugged Sally.

"Now that Joe's been bitten by the 'island bug', I think we might make the trip more often," Sally said.

With Aunt Sally lost in thought and Callie dozing off and on, the ride back to Columbia was quiet and uneventful. Because it was nearly eight o'clock, Joe dropped Callie off at home before taking Aunt Sally home.

4

Columbia 1964

Callie got off the school bus near her Aunt Sally's house. Today she was going to help her aunt get the back bedroom ready before Sally's son, Claude, came to visit. She frowned and crinkled her nose as the smoke from the mills filled her nostrils. *This place stinks. And all the dust from the red clay messes up everything.* Tall pine trees lining the narrow asphalt road offered little shade from the afternoon sun.

She tried not to think about her books biting into her arm as she continued down the road. *There'll be red welts and dents in my arm by the time I get there.* She puffed out a breath to move the hair away from her face. *It'll be busy moving the furniture, cleaning, and washing all the linens, but it's always so calm at Aunt Sally's. Not at all like home. Even though Dad's pretty mellow, Momma's so jittery, like something could set her off at any minute. I don't understand why she thinks something bad's going to happen all the time. Ah, there's the Simpson's house. Aunt Sally's is next.*

Callie knocked on the screen door after wiping her feet on the bristly welcome mat at the front door. "That you Callie?" her Aunt Sally called from the kitchen door at the end of the hall. "Come on in. The screen's unlocked." Expensive oriental rugs dotted the highly polished wood floors throughout the house. *Red clay would likely mar them for life.*

"Yes, ma'am. I'll set my books down and be right there." Callie paused for a moment to take off her shoes. *Dang it, I keep forgetting to bring an extra pair of slippers to leave here. I'll just go around in sock feet.*

She entered the black and white tiled kitchen and stopped to give her aunt a hug.

"Do you want something to drink before we get started?" Aunt Sally asked, looking up from the notebook where she wrote to-do lists and tracked her expenses. "I picked up some Cokes when Jolene took me into town today."

"Thank you. A Coke sounds good. Can I get anything for you?" Callie asked as she walked to the refrigerator. "These small bottles are so cute."

"No, I've got some tea here."

"What are we doing today." Callie sat down beside her aunt. Like her sister, Lydia, Sally had a wooden hutch with a matching table and several chairs in the kitchen.

"I thought we would do the bed linens today." Aunt Sally moved her notebook over so Callie could see the list. "I just have the bedspread on the bed right now. And I'd like to move the armchair and its table over by the window. There's a pretty view of the backyard from there. Oh, there's a floor lamp, too."

"Is that all we're moving?" Callie took a long drink of her Coke. *Aunt Sally takes care of most stuff around the house. I'm glad to help her since she's weak on her left side and carrying heavier stuff is hard for her.*

"Oh, yes, there's no need to rearrange the whole room. Besides, the chest and dresser are much too heavy for us to move. How is Joe doing? Did you guys go to the dance last weekend?"

"No, he's already graduated so he isn't allowed to be on school property." Her lips curved downward. "We went to the movies, instead. We got to go last year, though. Getting all dressed up is okay, but I can do without it." After finishing her Coke, she continued. "Besides, we're getting married after I graduate."

"I'm looking forward to your wedding." Seeing that Callie had finished her Coke, Sally brushed her dark hair off her forehead, stood, and picked up her cane from where it hung on the back of the chair. "We can get started if you're ready now."

Callie's feet slipped on the waxed tile floor when she stood up. Catching herself on the table, she laughed. "I've been meaning to bring a pair of slippers, but I keep forgetting."

She followed her aunt down the hall. Entering the bedroom, she began removing the pillows and the heavy chenille bedspread from the bed. "I'll put this in the washer and be right back."

"Wait just a minute," her aunt said turning to leave the room. Callie gathered the spread up to the edge of the bed and waited.

Her aunt returned with a pair of terry cloth slippers with rubber soles, the ones with elastic around the top so they do not slip off. "Here put these on. They're just an extra pair I have."

"Thank you." She put on the slippers before picking up the spread. "I'll get this started and be right back."

Callie easily moved the wingback chair, a tall floor lamp, and a table in front of the

window and began dusting. Aunt Sally placed items around the room and Callie took note of the little touches her aunt added to the room to make her guests comfortable. Matches sat in an ashtray on the table by the chair.

On the dresser, she had placed a small tray with tiny bottles of face cream, shampoo, and conditioner. A box of tissues sat beside a lamp on each of the nightstands. A few books graced the tall chest near the closet.

When she went to the linen closet in the hall, Callie inhaled deeply to capture the scent of lavender that permeated the space. Returning to the bedroom she asked her aunt. "How do you keep your linen closet smelling so nice?"

Aunt Sally smiled. "That's a trick I learned living on the island. Lavender sachets. If you aren't careful there, everything can get a musty smell, even if it doesn't mildew. My friend Alma and I used to make them."

Callie's eyes took on a dreamy look as she inhaled the delicate scent lingering on the bed sheets. "Can you buy them?"

"I expect so, but I have lavender growing in the backyard. I can tell you how to make them, but I'm not much with a needle. Can you sew?"

Callie's eyes sparkled. "Oh, yes. Momma started teaching me to sew when I was about ten."

"Okay, go ahead and put the sheets on the bed and I'll get one of the sachets for you. I'll show you how to dry the lavender once I go out and pick some."

"I'll put the spread in the dryer and then get the sheets." Sally was still outside when Callie returned to the kitchen. *She's been out there a while. Maybe I should go out and see if Aunt Sally needs help.*

"Aunt Sally, can I help out here?" Callie stopped beside the tall gray-green lavender plant.

"No thanks, I've got this. When Alex set up this bed for me, he created some nice stone paths that make it easy for me to walk around."

"The blooms are so delicate."

"They are, but it's the leaves that give us the wonderful scent." Sally plucked a few leaves and handed them to Callie. "Crush the leaves and smell them."

Callie followed her aunt's instructions and inhaled deeply. "Oh, that's really something. I think I will have to grow lavender when I have a garden of my own."

Sally's eyes danced as she watched Callie gently move the lavender plant so she could examine its base. "Oh, the main stems are really woody."

"They can be tricky to grow. But mostly lavender needs well-drained soil," Sally said grinning.

"Ah, I'm guessing you amended Columbia's native red clay."

"Yes. You dig a hole larger than the mature plant's root ball and fill it with a sandy loam. Once it gets going you prune it every year and that's that." Sally straightened up to her full five foot four height with a sigh and slipped her scissors into a pocket. "Let's go inside. I'm feeling a little stiff."

"I'll take the lavender inside if you'd like." Carefully Callie took the small bundle from her aunt.

"I'll get some string and join you at the kitchen table."

Entering the kitchen, they changed back into slippers. After placing the lavender on the kitchen table, Callie poured a glass of tea for her aunt and got another Coke for herself. Taking a chair at the table, she examined the small, fragrant bag her aunt had left there before going out into the yard. *You just sew these along three sides. Maybe add a bit of lace and a drawstring at the top. I think I'll make some to put in my hope chest.*

"Thank you for getting my tea." Sally sat beside Callie. "You'll have to tie the bundles since they're so small. My left hand doesn't work like it should. Once the lavender is in bundles, you hang it upside down to dry."

"That's so cool."

While they sat around the table, Aunt Sally told Callie about how she came to live on the island full time after her husband died. "Some of my views on feminism and racial equality put me at odds with our circle of friends and without Claude it was all meaningless to me anyway. When I decided to move to the island, Claude Junior and Alice decided to remain in Charleston with Claude's sister. That would keep them in the same prep school and the social circle they loved."

"It had to be hard, leaving your children like that." Callie's hand flew to her mouth, afraid she had offended her aunt. "I'm sorry. I didn't mean—"

Sally waved a hand at Callie, as if to brush away the comment. "No offense taken, It was hard, but I was often in Charleston or they were on the island. Anyway, my children were nearly grown, getting ready to enter college and already working in the family business. They had been interns since they entered high school. After I had my stroke, I was afraid to drive, and it was harder to get around."

Callie wasn't sure about all these revelations. *I never knew any of this. And what kind of business does her husband's family have? Must be pretty big.*

Sally paused a moment, absentmindedly rubbing her left hand. "So I decided to move here near your mother. She always looked after me when we were younger. But she's changed some since then." Sally frowned slightly. "Besides, I was never close to Claude's brothers and sister. Sometimes it's good to be with people who've known you all your life."

"I do remember running on the beaches there and the magnolias. Everything smelled so fresh," Callie said with a faraway look in her eyes. "It was great to go back to the island."

"It is a great place to live, but it has its drawbacks. You have to leave the island to do any major shopping. And then there are the hurricanes."

Callie stood up and rinsed her coke bottle before returning it to the carton under the sink. "I could sit here talking with you all day, but it's nearly supper time and I do have homework that's due tomorrow. I'll get the spread on the bed before I go, though."

A few minutes later, Aunt Sally walked her to the door. "Thanks for all your help today." Callie sat down to change her shoes. "Just put the slippers in the drawer there on the hall tree. That way they'll be waiting for you next time."

With her shoes changed, Callie hugged her aunt before picking up her books. "You're welcome. I'm glad to help out. I'll be back once your son leaves."

"I expect I'll be down soon to see your mother, but stop in anytime," Aunt Sally said as she opened the screen door.

"Okay, see you soon."

Callie smiled to herself as she walked the few short blocks home. Her thoughts kept returning to her visit to Caines Island with Aunt Sally. *It would be such a wonderful place to live. Being able to see all those birds every day: the herons, seagulls, and those cute little sandpipers bouncing along the edge of the water. All the magnolia trees.* Her binder pinched her arm and brought her back to the present as she turned onto the walk leading to her front porch.

5

Columbia 1965

Callie and her mother stood at the sink washing supper dishes. Waiting for her mother to wash a couple of things, she stared out the window over the sink. Her mother's vegetable garden filled most of the view, although you could see the corner of her dad's workshop and the black-eyed susans her mother had planted along its foundation. Her brother, Bobby, would be home from college tomorrow. Her mother had planned a big family supper. Of course, Aunt Sally and Joe would be there.

"Momma, is Susan coming?" Callie asked as she finished drying a plate and put it in the cabinet.

"I'm pretty sure she is. She'll want to see her parents, too." Her mother put another plate in the dish rack on the counter. Like everything else in the kitchen, it was bright yellow.

"Good. I like her a lot. What are we having for supper tomorrow?"

"Bobby asked me to fry chicken. So, we'll have rice, gravy, lima beans, and another vegetable. Not sure what."

"Sounds good to me. What's for dessert? Oh, be right back."

She took the towel which was more wet than dry and draped it across the washing machine. When she returned, she pulled another towel from a drawer and picked up where she left off. "I could make a chocolate cake tonight if you want me to."

Her mother put a couple of pots in the sink before answering. "That would be nice. Everyone loves your cakes. I'm sure we have everything for it."

The cake was in the oven when her dad came into the kitchen to let her know Joe was on the phone, no surprise, since he either came by or called most days. Callie sat down next to the small phone table and wondered why her parents never had an extension put in the kitchen. *It would be so much easier to talk there.*

"Hey, Joe," Callie said into the receiver.

"Hello there beautiful." She heard him say. Smiling, she shook her head, Joe always made her feel she was the most wonderful person on earth. They talked for a while and told each other about their day. "I've got a cake in the oven. It'll be done any minute now," she told him. After telling her he loved her and he'd be over after he went to the bank, Joe said goodbye.

Callie returned to the kitchen, took the cake out of the oven and put it on cooling racks. Then she began making the frosting. By the time she was cleaning the mixer, her mother joined her in the kitchen. "Did I hear the phone ring?" her mother asked as she sat down at the table and began fiddling with the placemat in front of her.

"Yes, ma'am, it was Joe telling me about the house they're building outside of town. A pretty big one apparently." Callie sat the bottom layer of the cake on the cake stand and began frosting its top.

"It's good things are going well since he decided to leave the mill. I'm not sure I understand him leaving something so secure, though." Her mother picked up the placemat and began pleating its edges. Soon it looked like a fan.

"I know, but he hates being cooped up inside all day. And now he can see what he's done in a day." Callie settled the top layer on the frosted bottom layer and began frosting the top of the cake. *Oh, Lordy. I hope we're not going to have 'the security conversation' again.*

"I like Joe a lot, but I think he should look at some of the older men in the neighborhood. Most of them, like your dad, have steady work and will have a pension." Her mother looked down at the mangled placemat in her hands and tried unsuccessfully to flatten it again, "Guess I'll go ahead and put out the other placemats." She stood and gathered the placemats on the table.

As her mother went into the laundry area, Callie shook her head. *Sometimes, I'm not sure Momma knows what she's doing when she does stuff like that, messing up a perfectly good placemat.*

Her mother returned to the kitchen, pulled another set of placemats from a drawer in the hutch, and continued as if she had never left the room. "A man's got to consider his family's future, that's all."

Callie stood at the counter with her back turned to her mother, frosting the sides of the cake. She blew out a small breath before answering. "He is. He's saved nearly everything since we became engaged, even though I haven't worn an engagement ring yet. Heck, he's still driving the same truck he bought when he first learned to drive." She put the cover on the finished cake and placed it on the hutch which sat along the narrow back wall of the kitchen.

"It's just something you should think about." Her mother moved closer to Callie and gave her a hug before leaving the kitchen. Pausing at the kitchen door, she looked back at Callie frowning. "I just want what's best for you."

"Okay, Momma. But I'm not changing my mind about Joe's and my future," she said as she returned to the sink. "I'll clean this up and study some in my room until Joe gets here. See you in the morning." Callie heard her mother's soft footsteps going down the hall toward her parent's bedroom.

At breakfast in the morning, Callie had been afraid her mother would start on Joe's job again, but she was in luck. Today, it was Bobby's turn to be the focus of her mother's unease while she and her parents sat around the table eating breakfast.

"I wish they could stay longer or at least have more time to travel. I worry about them being too tired while they're on the road." Callie's mother alternated between picking at her food and running a hand through her auburn hair.

"Don't fret so, Lydia. The drive from Charleston is not that long," Callie's dad said over a forkful of ham and eggs.

"Oh, I just feel nervous this morning." Her mother stood and picked up her plate and silverware, before continuing. "Callie, would you please clean up the kitchen? I think I need to take a pill and lie down before everyone gets here."

Callie and her dad finished breakfast in silence. She cleaned the kitchen while her dad went to mow the yard. Even though it was too early to start preparing supper, Callie took out quart jars of lima beans and green beans she and her mother had canned last year and set them on the counter. With the house ready for company, Callie went to her bedroom and worked on her assignment that was due Monday.

Callie's dad returned with Aunt Sally just about noon. Bobby and Susan pulled into the driveway shortly after. Callie bounded down the front porch steps to hug her big brother. Although he was six years older, they were very close. "So glad you're here." Callie hurried around the car to hug Susan. From the time Bobby and Susan began dating, Callie had felt they were the perfect couple. Susan fit in well with the family; she had a great sense of humor and her love for Bobby was obvious. She was in a program for social workers. Bobby was in a pre-med program at Charleston University on a scholarship.

"Where's Joe?" Bobby asked as everyone began gathering in the kitchen.

"He wanted to be here earlier, but his dad is working on the barn and needed his help," Callie told him.

Joe's dad worked at the mill too, but he had really wanted to be a farmer. After he inherited a house with some land from a distant uncle, Joe's dad moved the family out of the mill community and bought a couple of cows. By the time he retired in a few of years, he hoped the farm would be a going concern.

Callie, her mother, and Susan began putting together a lunch for everyone. They prepared a relish plate with fresh vegetables and bread and butter pickles that Callie and her mother had put up. There was homemade potato salad left from supper last night. Her dad came in to help and sliced the ham nice and thin, perfect for sandwiches.

Her mother looked over her shoulder. "Bob, we need a couple of extra chairs. I'm glad I left the extra leaf in after Christmas last year. Maybe, I'll just leave it in." Bobby helped his dad bring a couple more chairs to the table while Callie added more placemats.

Everyone had settled into their places when Callie heard someone pull into the driveway. "That must be Joe. Excuse me, I'll be right back."

Callie met Joe on the front porch for a hug and kiss before they joined the rest of the family. "You're just in time. Lunch is ready. Come on in; everyone is here."

In the kitchen, Joe and Callie sat down in their usual seats on her dad's left. "Hi, everybody. How was the trip, Bobby?" Joe waited for the bread and then began making a sandwich,

"Not too bad, we started out early," Bobby said after swallowing. Hey, Sis you're getting to be an old woman. Graduating in June and getting married in September."

He laughed when Callie threw her napkin at him. "Susan, have you set a date for your wedding?"

Susan shrugged. "I graduate in May, so probably the end of June or July next year. I have to talk to my parents though."

"Oh my, there's always so much happening with all these young people around." Aunt Sally smiled at her niece and nephew. "Helps me feel young."

The talk continued with plans around Callie's graduation. It would be just a small gathering with family and a few close friends. Although her mother wanted to do something more elaborate, Callie was insistent on the small event to save money for the wedding in September.

6

Caines Island 1969

Callie paused a moment to look at the herons soaring across the cloudy sky as she got out of the car. *We didn't have time for a walk this morning. There was just so much to do.* With Kimberly in her arms, she continued up the walk, made her way up the steps and onto the porch. Callie wore a wide-brimmed black hat with a short veil and a simple, black A-line dress. Her parents weren't far behind. At the front door, she turned and looked back at her parents. "I've got to feed Kimberly now. I'll be out in a few minutes."

Closing the door to the nursery, Callie laid Kimberly in the crib while she took off her hat and slipped out of her heels and dress. Picking up her daughter again, she relaxed in the rocking chair Joe had refinished for her. Cooing to her daughter, she settled Kimberly at her breast.

"Okay, baby girl, it's just you and me now. I think we should stay right here in this house. What do you think?" Callie looked at her daughter intent on nursing. "I really didn't think you'd have an answer for me. But that's okay, I'll figure it out." Once Kimberly had her fill, she settled the baby in the basket woven by her neighbor, Alma. Callie dressed again and took her daughter into the living room.

She settled Kimberly's basket near a window, so she'd be in the sunshine. *Wow, everyone must have left right after us.* She began making her way through the house and expressing her appreciation for their condolences. *I didn't realize Joe and I knew so many people. And all this* *food. I think someone's been stopping by every day. A*t one point, she tried to take a tray back to the kitchen when her friend, Josie, took it from her. "Not today," she said. "Let your friends take care of you today. Go sit down."

Joe's parents left around four. They would stay overnight in a hotel in Mt. Pleasant before returning to Columbia tomorrow morning. Their departure started a steady stream of people getting on with their lives, and by five o'clock everyone had left except for her parents and Josie. Callie's dad was cuddling Kimberly on the couch. Callie, her mother, and Josie began cleaning up. "There's so much food." Callie's eyes grew wide as she looked at the table and counters laden with food. "I'm not sure I'll be able to eat all this food before it turns."

"You could freeze the ham and use it later in beans or soup," her mother said.

"Okay, but I've used the last of my freezer containers. We'll wrap the ham and put it in the fridge until later," Callie said before turning her attention to the leftover chicken. "Oh, and I'll freeze the plain vegetables, too," she added as she put the chicken in the refrigerator.

"Make a list of what you need in town. We can get it tomorrow since we aren't leaving until Monday morning," her mother said as she filled the sink with hot soapy water.

Josie organized dishes for Callie's mother to wash and turned to Callie and asked. "What happened with Joe's truck?"

"When the dump truck crashed, the wall crumbled onto the truck. Joe's supervisor thinks it's totaled. I'll have to see what the insurance company says," Callie said as she began to dry and put away dishes.

"Well, I have our truck a couple of times a week," Josie said putting containers of food away before wiping down the counters. "You can ride into town with me."

"Thanks, Josie," Callie said putting away the last of the dishes. "I'll keep that in mind."

With the kitchen and living room cleaned, Josie said good night. Not long after, Callie's parents went to bed. Kimberly was already asleep in the bassinet in Callie's room. Callie changed into her nightgown and curled up, hugging Joe's pillow. *I'm so tired. I'm not sure how to go on from here without Joe. I wish he were here.* Tears rolled down her cheeks. Callie made no effort to stop them and eventually fell asleep.

After feeding Kimberly and getting her settled in the crib the next morning, Callie quickly got a shower before her parents woke up. *Today is going to be like yesterday, so once I'm dressed, I'll work on breakfast for us.* Her parents tended to be early risers, so Callie started warming some ham and making biscuits. *Momma will probably fuss about me not letting her fix breakfast. She doesn't seem to realize staying busy keeps me from falling apart. And I just can't do that, I've got Kimberly to think of.*

That afternoon several more people stopped by to pay their respects. Alma and Louise oversaw setting out more food, while Brenda and Josie made sure everyone was comfortable and had something to drink. *Brenda and Josie are such wonderful friends.* Callie smiled wanly as people offered their condolences and promises of assistance should she need something. *You can't give me what I need most---Joe. I appreciate all this but why can't they see I'm lost?* She let out a deep sigh. *I can't stay lost though. I've got to pull myself together for Kimberly.* With another deep sigh, she looked up at Max as he handed her a plate filled with tidbits from the kitchen.

"You need to eat, Callie." His usual grinning face was somber. "Got to keep your strength up for your little one."

"I know but—" Callie looked down at her lap.

"Come on now. This broccoli salad is really good." Max sat next to Callie until she started to eat. "Ah, I think Kimberly's awake. Maybe I can hold her a while before your mother gets to her." Max laughed softly and he stood up.

Somehow Callie made it through the day. That night while she sat rocking Kimberly before putting her in the bassinet, Callie felt some of her strength returning. She didn't know how she would work things out so she could stay on the island, but she knew she would.

Monday afternoon, Callie stood by the car while her mother rolled down the

window, "Please think about coming back to Columbia? I could help more with Kimberly."

"I don't think so, Momma," Callie answered. "Kimberly and I have a home and friends here."

Her dad put a hand on her mother's arm to forestall further comment. Leaning forward to talk around her, "It's too soon to be making any decisions Callie. Just let us know how we can help." Giving his wife a kiss on the cheek before he sat back in the seat, Callie's dad waved and backed down the driveway.

7

Caines Island July 1965

Callie plopped onto the porch swing and watched the few cars moving slowly along the street in front of the house. She and her mother had just had another argument about having the wedding this year. *I've already agreed to wait until the fall. If I did what I wanted, we'd have gotten married in June. I stayed in school like I promised. Why does she want me to wait another year? Joe and I have waited long enough as far as I can see. I wish Joe would get here.* With her temper calmed, Callie went back inside.

As she closed the front door, her dad looked at her over the morning paper. "When is Joe picking you up?" He folded the paper and let it fall to his lap.

"He'll be here soon. We'll pick up Aunt Sally before going to the island and stay with her while we look for an apartment in Charleston."

"Okay. I'm sure you guys can find something. Especially since you're starting early."

Callie looked toward the kitchen trying to see where her mother was and plopped on the couch. "Hopefully, we'll find something with a lease ending in the fall. And Joe wants to do some small repairs for Aunt Sally while we're there." She looked at the floor and studied the carpet. "Do you know why Momma wants us to wait until next June to get married?"

"She's just having a hard time realizing you've grown up, especially since you two are moving to Charleston." Her dad reached over and patted her knee. "She'll come around. You know she likes Joe. Don't worry honey, everything will work out."

Hearing Joe's truck in the driveway, Callie stood up and leaned over to hug her dad. "I love you, Dad." Straightening up, she asked, "Where's Mom?"

"Probably out back in the garden." Her dad folded the paper in quarters to finish later.

She got up, walked to the door, and opened it. "Hey, Joe," Callie said, giving him a kiss before walking toward the kitchen. "I'll say good-bye to Momma before we go."

"All right, I'll wait here with your dad." Joe sat down on the couch. Within a few minutes, Callie returned and hugged her dad again before they left.

Arriving on the island, Callie and Joe unloaded the car while Sally went to see Alma. Putting her suitcase in the bedroom, Callie joined Joe in the kitchen to see what he was going to fix this weekend. "Are you ready to head into town?"

"Yeah, I've got my list. There's a lot of stuff that needs to be done here. Some of it's small stuff, so maybe I can help with that." He held her hand as they left the kitchen.

"It's nice of Aunt Sally to let us stay here and use her car to go to Charleston," Joe said as he backed out of the driveway.

Callie waved to Aunt Sally and Alma, who were sitting on Alma's porch. "It's so peaceful here. Are you sure you don't mind moving to Charleston?" Callie looked at Joe as she slid closer to him on the seat.

"No, I didn't really like working at the mill. I'll find a job in construction down here. Since I quit the mill, I've been working with Steve Williams. You know he'll give me a good reference." Joe smiled, but kept his eyes on the road. "Everyone says construction is booming in Charleston."

"Okay, I didn't think you were doing this just because I want to. But I had to be sure." Callie rested her head on his shoulder for a moment. She sat up straighter and continued. "You know I can get a job, too. I'm sure I won't make as much as you do, but it'd help us save some money." *We never really talked about me working, but most couples we know started out with both people working. At least 'til the babies start coming.*

"Yeah, you can do that if you want." Joe patted her leg. "Hopefully, you won't have to work when we have kids."

"Okay, then. When we get to Charleston, we need to stop and get a couple of newspapers." Callie stretched to look at the marshland when they crossed the bridge into Mount Pleasant. *It's so pretty and green with all the tall grasses. Is that a heron?*

"When we're through looking at apartments, we can go by the hardware store and Piggly Wiggly." He took his eyes off the road briefly to smile at Callie. "What are you looking at out there?"

"Pretty sure it was a heron. They're so big. Can't wait until we get a chance to walk on the beach." Callie had a huge grin on her face as she turned to look at Joe.

"We can take picnic lunches to the beach. Didn't I see a small store there?" His grin matched Callie's. "I liked walking there and seeing all the birds, too, especially the sandpipers."

Stopping at a gas station, Callie picked up a couple of newspapers and a Coke for each of them while Joe waited for the attendant to fill up the car and clean the windshield. After she got in the car, Joe pulled away from the gas pumps and parked beside the building. Taking a newspaper, they began looking through a it, circling any apartments that fell within their budget.

They were nearly ready to give up when they found the apartment on Morris Street. They parked out front of a two story, gray stucco building with wide porches that ran along the length of the building. Black wrought iron railings lined the porches and stairwell.

Callie said hopefully, "It looks like the outside's been maintained."

Joe nodded. "What apartment are we supposed to go to, so we can see the one for rent?"

Callie looked at the ad again. "Number eight." She squinted to get a closer look at the apartment numbers. "That's it. On the right, last one on the end."

Joe got out of the car, stretched, and waited for Callie to get out. "Okay, let's go," he said.

"Hope the apartment is downstairs. I'd hate to climb these steps every time I went somewhere." Callie paused a moment to get a tissue from her purse and wipe the sweat from her forehead when they reached the second floor.

"Agreed." Joe led the way to the superintendent's apartment. Within a few minutes, they were downstairs looking at a corner apartment. It had a small galley kitchen, a living room/dining room combination, a bathroom, and a bedroom. All the rooms were painted a light brown color and the living room/dining room was had chair railing. The chair railing and molding around the windows and doors where painted white.

"Take a look out back, the shed has a place where you can park your truck. There's one space for every apartment. I gotta check something in another apartment. I'll be right back."

Callie ran her fingers through her damp hair. "It's kind of small, but we don't need much room for just the two of us." She smiled as she walked through the apartment again and stopped by the back door, thinking of ways she could make it cozier.

"Are you sure you like it?" Joe stepped up behind her circling his hands around her waist and pulling her closer. "Don't just settle. We could come down and look again."

"No, I like it. I know it's an older building, but they've kept it up. I like the molding around the windows, doors, and the chair railing in the living room. And look, there's a back porch too." She turned to give him a hug. "Let's see if we can get it."

When they talked with the superintendent, it was apparent he wanted to rent the apartment right away. The couple was obviously disappointed. They were nearly back at the car when Joe handed Callie the keys and asked her to wait in the car. As Joe walked back to the apartment building, the superintendent paused at the bottom of the stairs.

"Did you guys change your mind?" he asked seriously. "I can't rent it to an unmarried couple, you know."

"I know. Like I said we're getting married in September. Could you hold off renting the place until tomorrow? I want to talk over something with Callie first."

"Okay, you seem like nice folks. Call me tomorrow."

Driving back to Caines Island, Joe outlined his plan of renting the apartment and finding work in Charleston. "Steve might want me to stay until we finish this house, but we should be through in a couple of weeks. We've saved enough for two month's rent. I'll be working long before the third month's rent is due."

"I don't want us to be apart." Callie twisted her fingers together in her lap. "Maybe Aunt Sally will make another trip soon."

"Honey, I don't want us to be apart either. It will just be three months. I'll call and come home some weekends." Joe put an arm around her shoulder and his voice became more urgent. "You saw how few decent apartments there are that we can afford. Come on Callie."

She sniffled and tears gathered in the corners of her eyes. "It is a nice apartment." Callie washed her hands together as she sat silently staring out of the window. *It does make some sense. I just had this picture of us being together over the summer and then getting an apartment. It's not like he's going across the country.* "I guess I can stand it if you can. We can take some measurements tomorrow and I'll make curtains while you're gone."

Joe gave her shoulders a squeeze and took his arm from around her to focus on driving. "I'll call from Aunt Sally's when we get back and we can come back tomorrow. That super liked us a lot."

8

Columbia 1965

Callie sat at Aunt Sally's kitchen table tracing the wood grain patterns with a finger while she waited for her cousins, Claude and Alice, to arrive. *Why did she have to die? I was just getting to know her as a person. It's too stifling in here.* She wiped tears from her eyes with the back of her hand.

Uncertain about what she was supposed to do while she waited, Callie went out onto the front porch, sat in a rocking chair, and pulled her hair back into a ponytail. *Strange to think I've got cousins I hardly know. Yeah, we'd get together sometimes when they came to visit Aunt Sally, but we don't really have much in common, I guess. They were busy running the family business. I'm not even sure what that is. Funny, they don't have a key to this house.* A bright red Posche pulling into the driveway interrupted Callie's thoughts.

Callie stood and walked down the steps to greet her cousins as they stepped out of the car. "Hope your drive was okay? Sorry you had to travel at a time like this."

"It was fine, the car is pretty comfortable. I'm Claude. It's been so long; not sure you'd remember. You must be Callie, and this is my sister Alice," the short, stocky young man said as he reached out to shake Callie's hand. *They're just a few years older than me. Why are they here alone?*

"Yes, it has been a few years since we last got together. Come inside out of this heat. Sorry my mother isn't here, but she's taking this hard." Callie turned to walk back inside the coolness of the house.

Inside she offered tea or a soda. Alice and Claude sat on the sofa in the living room. "No, thank you," Alice said setting her handbag next to her.

Callie couldn't help but notice the interlocking C's near the heel of Alice's flats as she sat in a nearby armchair, looking at her cousins. *How different from Aunt Sally. She bought really nice stuff, but not so obvious. And the miniskirt with a poor boy sweater. Alice is going to burn up, even if her skirt is shorter than my shorts.*

"No, I'm fine right now. Just tell me where Mother's..." He paused and cleared his throat, "Mother's body is?"

He spoke quickly, nearly running the words together so Callie was surprised when her cousins stared at her waiting for an answer. "Oh, she's at Wilson's funeral home. They know the services are taking place in Charleston." Suddenly she could only focus on the fact that both of her cousins' outdoor shoes were resting on the Persian rug. Aunt Sally had always changed shoes when she got home. She even carried a pair of slippers when she visited Callie's family. With an effort she refocused. "Is there anything I can help you with?"

"No. Or at least not right now. I'll go through some things and let you know," Alice said as she gracefully stood and walked down the hallway toward the kitchen.

Callie looked at Claude uncertainly. "I brought a few things for sandwiches and put them in the refrigerator. Of course, you're welcome to come to supper if you'd like. I left our address and phone number on a pad in the kitchen. The house key is there, too." Callie walked down the hall to get her purse from the kitchen and stopped in the living room to say goodbye to Claude before leaving.

"Callie, thanks for everything. We'll probably just hang around here after we go to the funeral home. Our uncle has already talked to them. I just have to give them the card to imprint. I'll be sure to let you know about the service and things. I know you were incredibly special to Mother." Claude looked around the tidy room.

"Thank you. I appreciate that. Call if you need anything." Holding back tears, Callie walked into the hall, changed out of her slippers, and let herself out into the oven that was July's heat.

At home, Callie plopped on the porch swing and stared out at her mother's purple coneflowers under the pine trees. *Everything is changing so fast. Joe's in Charleston. Aunt Sally's gone. Now I wonder if Momma is right. Maybe we should delay the wedding. But we've put deposits on everything. I'm not sure what's the right thing to do.* Callie shook herself and went inside; her mother needed to know there wouldn't be extra people for supper tonight.

A few days later, Alice called and asked Callie to come to Aunt Sally's house before lunch; she and Claude had a few things they'd like to talk over with her. By ten that morning the sun was scorching the earth. Callie dreaded the short walk to her aunt's house.

She was changing out of the halter top she had been wearing when her mother knocked on the door. "Sweetie, I'm going to the grocery store. Why don't I drop you off on the way?"

Buttoning her blouse, Callie grinned at her mother. "That would be fantastic. It's blazing hot out there today. I'm nearly ready to go."

After waving goodbye to her mother, Callie walked up the driveway with a lump in her throat. *They'll be selling this house. It'll be so weird for someone else to live here.* Callie had just a short wait after knocking on the door before Alice opened it, dressed in flared jeans and a silk top. Alice's long dark hair hung straight down her back and she wore a headband that matched her blouse. Claude wore flared jeans and a sweater much like the one his sister wore yesterday. "Hey. Thanks for coming. Would you like something to drink? Claude's in the kitchen. I think there's Coke in the refrigerator."

Callie noticed boxes in some of the rooms as she followed Alice down the familiar hallway. *Even though her things are still here, I can't feel Aunt Sally*. "A Coke would be nice, thank you," Callie said when they entered the kitchen.

Claude stood up and offered her a seat at the kitchen table while Alice poured the Coke into a glass with ice. Giving Callie her drink, Alice joined them at the table. "I've been able to sort out some things we'll have shipped back to Charleston, but there's still a lot here that could be put to good use. Claude and I would like you and your parents to take anything you'd like."

"Wow, thanks. I hadn't even." Callie paused trying not to cry.

Claude jumped in. "Once you and your parents have made your choices, we've contracted with an auction house to collect the rest. Mother had nice things here, but she gave her truly priceless, memorable things to us when she closed the Charleston house and they've been stored in a company warehouse until we're ready for them."

"And a lot of the stuff here will be hopelessly outdated once we get our own places." Alice looked down at her nails.

Blinking, Callie took a sip of her soda. "That's awful generous. I'll let my mother know."

"We've listed or boxed things we'd like to keep. Uncle Michael will contact a real estate agent when the house is empty," Alice paused and dabbed at her eyes with a tissue.

"Anyway," Claude said. "Could you keep an eye on the place until it's sold? At least, until you get married. September, isn't it?" He picked up his glass and took a long drink before looking back at Callie.

"About that, I'm not sure Joe and I should still get married in September." Callie shifted in her chair.

"Of course you should," Claude sat his glass down and looked at Callie intently.

"You've already sent out the invitations and put down deposits," Alice chimed in, patting an imaginary stray hair back in place. "Mother wouldn't want it any other way. She often told us how happy she was around you two. How you reminded her of us."

"Well, if you're sure it wouldn't be disrespectful." Callie sipped her Coke. "Okay, I can look after the house. I know where she keeps stuff, so it will be ready for showing."

"We'd like to have the service next Saturday. Will it be a problem for your family to be there?" *Claude seems to be ticking things off a list. I forgot Aunt Sally told me he was going to be a lawyer.*

"No. Just give us the details; we'll be there. My brother is in school there, University of Charleston, Medical School." Callie gave them a small smile as she thought of her brother with pride.

Alice got up, walked to the counter, and returned with a housekey. "We had a couple of extra ones made. Here's one for you."

Callie lifted one hip away from the chair and she slipped the key into the pocket of her shorts. "How much longer will you guys be here?"

Claude looked at Alice before answering, "We'll leave tomorrow morning early. I have to attend a business meeting Monday. It can't be rescheduled"

Callie finished her Coke and walked around the house with her cousins so that she understood what it was they wanted shipped. On the front porch, they chatted about Aunt Sally for a while. Without much more to say, Callie thanked them again and turned to walk home.

9

Caines Island/Columbia 1965, A Week Later

Callie sat in the kitchen at Aunt Sally's island house. Her parents had dropped her off there following the funeral service. Despite the fact Aunt Sally had deeded the house to her in the will, Callie couldn't think of it as hers. It just seemed too miraculous. *Maybe one day, Joe and I can live here with our children.*

After changing into shorts and a loose top, Callie closed up the house and walked down to the shore. She felt her sadness easing a little as she passed by sea oats dancing in the light breeze. The sound of waves crashing onto the shore amplified the dismay she felt about not knowing her aunt better. In the distance, she could see the sandpipers hopping about while they searched for their midday meal.

As she passed the dunes and reached the water's edge, she took off her flip-flops. She loved feeling the moist sand squishing between her toes. *Strange how little I know about Aunt Sally, even after all the time we spent together. I might have learned more, but Momma was uncomfortable enough at the service, so we made our apologies and didn't go to the wake at Michael's. I still don't know what their family business is. Claude called here to tell us about the will. Aunt Sally leaving me the house and enough money for Bobby to finish medical school was something none of us dreamed of. I've never met anyone as secretive about their past as Momma and Aunt Sally.* After a short while, she made her way to warmer, dryer sand and plopped to the ground, mesmerized by the ceaseless movement of the waves at high tide. After watching the waves for a few minutes, Callie's chest heaved with a sigh and she stood, brushed sand off her feet and put on her flip-flops. *I'd better get back to the house. Joe will be here soon.*

Callie was nearly at the porch when she saw Alma waving. "Come have a glass of tea," she called from the porch next door. "Your young man isn't here yet."

With a wave Callie made her way across the yard, looking back to get a good look at the house. She hadn't noticed how rundown things had gotten. Holes pocked what little screen remained on the porch. The white paint was dingy and the black shutters faded. *I know the inside needs painting and something's off with the plumbing. Well, one thing I know for sure, you don't get anything without hard work.* Climbing the steps to Alma's porch, Callie put remodeling out of her mind. "Tea sounds really good. I took a walk not thinking about how hot it is."

Alma nodded and her jet black hair fell forward against the coppery skin of her face before she flipped it back over her shoulder. "It is hot for sure. But you know there's a general store near the pavilion. Pete, Pete Jenkins, is open most days." Despite years of hard work, Alma stood nearly as tall as Callie and had a self-confident, regal air.

"Ah, I remember now. But I didn't have any money in my pocket anyway." Callie followed Alma inside. "It's nice and cool in here. Do the ceiling fans do all that?"

They were in the kitchen now. Alma paused as she took a pitcher of tea from the refrigerator. "Nah, you got to open your windows a little bit at the top and bottom." She took two tall glasses from a cabinet. "It keeps the air flowing."

"That's good to know." Callie took a long drink of tea.

Alma put the iced tea back in the refrigerator. "Let's go back out on the porch. I've got the fans going out there, too. Then you'll see your young man when he comes."

The two women sat under the porch's ceiling fan and traded stories about Aunt Sally and talked about the service today. Alma, Louise, and Max had stopped in briefly at the wake at Michael's, Callie didn't learn anything new about her aunt. They also exchanged phone numbers. When Joe's truck pulled into the driveway next door, Callie stood, ready to take her glass inside.

"Just leave that with me." Alma took Callie's glass. "I'll keep an eye on the place for you like I did for Sally."

"Thanks, Alma. I'm not sure when we'll get back. We'd still like to see you, Max, and Louise at the wedding, of course." Alma nodded and Callie bounced down the steps and hurried across the yard to meet Joe.

After getting her purse and the clothes she had worn this morning and closing up the house again, Joe and Callie started the journey back to Columbia. Lost in thought, she was unusually quiet until they were about an hour from home. "You know, I had no idea Aunt Sally would leave me the house on Caines Island. I'd like us to live there one day." Callie kept her eyes focused on her lap.

Joe looked over at her for a moment. "Well, it would take a lot to make it ready to live in full time." He wrinkled his nose as he thought. "I'm not sure the wiring is safe anymore. Then there's the money. I can do a lot, but I don't know anything about wiring."

Callie shifted in her seat to look at Joe. "I know. We have to take the repairs slow. I wanted to be sure you agreed with me"

"I get it. And this house is special to me, too. We can work on it bit by bit. Besides, it would take us a long time to save enough to buy a house." Joe patted Callie's thigh. "If we're careful with our money, we can do a lot ourselves."

"When I move to Charleston, I'll get a job too. I wish you didn't have to go back tomorrow. Things aren't the same without you there. And now without Aunt Sally, there's really not much for me to do." She slumped in the seat, staring out at the tall pine trees lining both sides of the road.

"Me, too." Joe squeezed her hand. "But you'll be busy planning the wedding and getting Aunt Sally's house in Columbia ready to be sold."

"I know. Alice and Claude want me to get to that right away. They seem to want to sell the house as fast as possible. Looks to me they could be more respectful and wait just a little longer." Callie sighed and shifted around in her seat trying to find a more comfortable position.

"From the looks of her children's clothes and cars, she had more money than she ever let on." Joe grinned. "Although it was plain, she had more money than any of us."

She nodded her head thoughtfully. "You're right about that, but she never lorded it over anyone. Claude kept saying something about probate and getting things settled to avoid tax problems. I don't know." Callie stifled a yawn.

Joe patted the seat next to him. "Curl up and take a nap. You've been going like crazy. I'll wake you up before we get to your house." She curled up on the seat and drifted off to sleep.

Callie opened her eyes slowly. *Where am I?* Without moving, she blinked and inhaled Joe's scent with a deep breath. *Oh, we must be nearly home.* She slid out from under his arm, careful not to bump the steering wheel, and sat up. Stretching, she grinned at him. "That was a good idea. I didn't realize I was so tired."

"We're almost at our turn-off. Should we stop and get a burger or something?"

"No. Momma and Dad will have something."

When they got to Callie's house, her dad was in the kitchen. "Hey guys. How was the trip? Are you ready to eat?" He got up from the table, walked toward the refrigerator before moving out of Callie's path and veering off to the sink.

"Don't worry about it, Dad. I'll get something together for us." Callie peered into the refrigerator. "Where's Momma, anyway?"

Looking out of the window over the kitchen sink, he answered. "She went to bed early. Travel, the funeral, it all took a lot out of her. Then the Stevens and the Jenkins came by with platters. Glad we're both home to help her out."

Callie pressed her lips into a tight line as she started putting the platters on the table, along with some things leftover from condolence visits last Friday. "I'll do whatever I can, Dad." Looking at Joe who stood leaning in the kitchen doorway, she continued. "How about some fried chicken and potato salad."

Joe took a few steps into the kitchen. "That sounds good. I hope it's my mom's potato salad. I'll get the plates. Mr. Parsons, are you going to join us?"

"I think I will," her dad replied. "I'll get the silverware and napkins."

The three of them ate in silence for a few minutes. Wiping his mouth, her dad sat back from the table. "Not to be disrespectful, but have you thought about what to do with the island house?"

"Eventually, we want to live in it." Callie grinned before taking a bite of potato salad.

Joe shrugged. "It will take a while. There's a lot we need to do, like wiring and replacing siding, things Aunt Sally wasn't able to get to. I helped her with small things when we went down, but she had trouble getting contractors for the bigger stuff." Joe shrugged again.

Her dad nodded. "I know. She used to talk about how handy you were and how much she appreciated your help."

They talked a little longer before Joe stood up, "Callie, I hate to go, but I should get to my parents'. I'll stop by after church tomorrow and maybe go up to Aunt Sally's with you for a little bit before I go back."

Callie got up from the table and looked at her dad. "I'll get the kitchen after I walk Joe out."

On the porch, Callie leaned into Joe's warm embrace as he nuzzled her hair. "It's probably a good thing I'm going back tomorrow," he said huskily.

"Hmm," Callie murmured. "Why did we agree to wait?" She giggled and moved back a little. "Well, nothing to be done about it now." She tilted her head up for a kiss.

After another longing embrace, Callie moved away from Joe while still holding his hand. "I'd better let you go before Dad comes out here to check on us."

"Yeah. Or the neighbors start coming outside to see the show." Joe laughed and squeezed her hand before turning to go. "I'll see you tomorrow."

Callie sat down on the porch swing to settle herself, knowing her dad would notice if she went inside all flustered. Their sense of propriety and fear of pregnancy had stopped them from 'going all the way' before. *It's just a couple of months until the wedding. Still, we've waited this long. Might as well stay the course.*

Callie ate a quick breakfast before her mother got up. *Dad's already at work. No sense getting Momma started about our keeping the house. I heard enough of that last night. Even though we lived on the island before I started school, she seems to have something against it. The movers are coming to pick up the things Alice and Claude wanted. I brought the thermos from Aunt Sally's home, so I'll take some tea to the house and maybe a couple of pimento cheese sandwiches. I'd better make another pitcher of tea before I go, though.*

After putting water on the stove to boil, Callie quickly washed her dishes from breakfast and put them in the dish drainer. *I'll dry them and put them away after I get dressed.* Moving the boiling water off the burner, Callie put tea bags in the pot to steep.

Quietly she returned to her room and pulled on a pair of shorts and a loose, sleeveless top. Slipping her feet into her favorite Keds, she felt ready to face the day.

With a sigh, she returned to the kitchen. *I'm not looking forward to today; there's not much actual work left to be done there. The movers are coming, and I've got a few things to pack.* Within a few minutes, she had tea made and put away the morning's dishes. Grabbing the thermos and the bag with her sandwiches, she made her way to Aunt Sally's house. She crinkled her nose as the breeze carried smoke from the mill her way.

Once inside Aunt Sally's house, Callie slipped off her Keds and put on her slippers like she usually did. She laughed to herself. *I rolled up the rugs in the hall yesterday, but wearing my slippers will keep the floors clean.* In the kitchen, Callie sat the thermos on the counter and her lunch in the refrigerator before turning her attention to the legal pad with the lists of where her aunt's possessions would wind up.

The sound of air brakes echoed along the quiet street announcing the moving truck's arrival. Callie went to the front door to greet the movers - a driver and two helpers. She walked them through the house and showed them the tags which indicated what they would pack and load today. With their instructions clear, the movers quickly gathered supplies from the truck and went to work. Two men began wrapping furniture in large, quilted blankets. The third man took wrapping paper and boxes into the dining room to start packing the things in the china hutch. They politely declined Callie's offer of iced tea.

In the kitchen, Callie began looking through the cabinets. *I know Claude and Alice said I should take anything Joe and I could use, but it seems weird to be looking through her stuff like this.* Tentatively, she selected a set of glasses and wrapped them in the newspapers she had saved. With the glasses safely ensconced in one of the boxes she had gotten from the grocery store, Callie continued to explore the cabinets. She already had the Fiesta dishes in the Caines Island house and felt sure they would be getting a set of dishes as a wedding present, so she left those for the auction house. Seeing the Revere ware with its shiny copper bottoms, Callie breathed a thank you to her aunt. She began placing the cookware on the counter. *This stainless steel will last forever and there's more than I could afford to buy. Heck, I could cook a Thanksgiving dinner and still not run out of pots.* Carefully, with newspaper between each pot, she nested the saucepans, double boilers, steamers, stock pots, and Dutch ovens into boxes.

Harry, the mover working in the dining room, came into the kitchen to let Callie know they were taking a break for lunch. "We all brought our lunch. Okay if we eat on the porch?"

"Sure, there's still a table out back." Callie pointed to the thermos. "There's still plenty of tea. It's been really hot here this week."

"Thanks, we might have some later." Harry left to get his lunch and tell the others where they could eat.

Her stomach rumbled and Callie looked down at her hands covered in ink from the papers. *Bet it's all over my face, too. I'll go clean up and eat.*

With lunch over, Callie packed a few more items. By mid-afternoon, even with a couple of short breaks to cool off with iced tea, the movers had loaded the truck and were preparing to leave. Harry met her on the front porch and handed her a clipboard. "If you'd sign here, ma'am." He pointed to a line at the bottom of the page and handed her a pen. "You'll have to press down hard. There are three copies of each page."

"All right." Callie signed each page and returned the clipboard and pen.

Harry took the pages she signed from the clipboard and then stuck it under his arm while separating the pages. "These are your copies. Have a good day." Harry went down the driveway and joined his coworkers in the truck.

Callie walked through the house; it seemed odd to her that so many of her aunt's belongings would wind up with strangers. Joe would be home this weekend and they would remove the pieces they wanted along with the boxes she had packed. Callie would have liked to have kept her aunt's dining room furniture, but there was no way it would fit in the Charleston apartment or the house on Caines Island. *I guess the next thing on the list is for Eli's auction house to come out next week. Everything is moving so fast.*

Pausing on the porch after locking the front door, Callie noticed dark clouds gathering. *Looks like thunderstorms this afternoon.* Her eyes were misty as she contemplated life without Aunt Sally. *Well, I'd better get moving before the rain comes in.*

That weekend, Callie and Joe moved their things from Aunt Sally's house and stored them in his parents' barn, so her house could be cleaned once the auction house picked up the items remaining there.

"Joe, I really like this kitchen table and chairs. The oak is so pretty. If I put cushions in the chairs, they'd be a little more comfortable. Maybe we can use it as a dining room table," Callie said while they carried the table into the barn. She slowed down and began swiveling her head around while she tried to see where they would put it.

"We've got to go further back, Callie," Joe said as her steps began to slow even more. "Dad's got a storage area away from the animals."

"All right, honey. I should have let you go in first." She tilted her head, shrugged, and began to walk more quickly.

After setting the table down, Joe grimaced slightly. "I know this won't fit in the apartment and I'm not sure where we'll put it in the island house."

"I'm hoping we can have a dining area in the living room. The hutch that goes with this is so nice." Callie grinned sheepishly. "I hope we can work it out somehow. I almost feel bad I didn't leave it for the auction house now." She walked around the table to stand beside Joe.

"Nah, honey. We'll figure out a way to work it in somehow." He put an arm around her shoulders and gave her a squeeze. "It's really cool that we get to start out with so many family things."

She leaned her head against his shoulder for a moment and then tousled his curly dark hair before moving away from him. "I guess it's time to get everything else in."

With everything moved into the barn, Callie and Joe went into the house for supper. Washing her hands at the kitchen sink, Callie asked. "Mrs. Stevens, is there something I can do to help with supper?"

Melinda Stevens turned from the stove to smile at Callie. She was tall with curly black hair. For as long as Callie could remember, Joe's mother had always been slender. "You can set the table. Everything is ready to put on the table when Joe Senior comes in."

"Yes ma'am. I'll do that." With long familiarity, Callie gathered dishes and silverware before setting the table.

"How's the wedding planning going?" Melinda, Joe's mother, began putting food into serving dishes.

"It's going pretty good. I've got a fitting scheduled at the end of the week," Callie said as she placed the last of the silverware on the table. "I just wish Joe didn't have to go back to Charleston."

"I know it's hard, but you two are made for each other. Oh, did Joe tell you, we're reserving the banquet room at The Jefferson for your rehearsal dinner?" Joe's mother asked as she began bringing food to the table.

"Oh, wow. Thank you. That'll be really nice. They have such good food." Callie smiled. She was glad Joe's parents seemed to like her. Callie had heard older girls talk about mothers who resented their son's wives, but she didn't think that would be a problem with Mrs. Stevens.

Joe and his father came into the kitchen. "Melinda, you've done it again. Perfect timing. I don't know how you do it." Mr. Stevens stopped beside his wife and gave her a kiss. "Callie, glad you could join us tonight." Joe moved to stand beside Callie.

"Thanks, Mr. Stevens. I appreciate your letting us store things in the barn until we can get them moved to Charleston."

"Callie, you're part of this family. It's what we do for each other," his dad said with a wave of his hand. He was a tall, stocky man, not overweight, just muscular.

"Let's all sit down before the food gets cold," Joe's mom said as she took her seat to the right of his dad who sat at the end of the table. Joe sat at the other end of the table and Callie sat across from Joe's mom.

Over supper, the four of them talked about plans for the wedding. Callie and Joe expressed their appreciation for being given not only the island house, but many of the things from Aunt Sally's Columbia house as well. When supper was over, Joe and his dad went back to the barn to check on a cow. "I'll be back to take you home soon, Callie."

"Okay, I've got to help your mom clean up first anyway."

10

Columbia September 1965

Dark slate gray thunderclouds swept across the sky as Callie sat on the porch watching the rain fall in slanting sheets. Even the coneflowers seemed to be shrinking as if trying to avoid the heavy rainfall. *This rain needs to stop soon. Susan's coming and we're supposed to do the final fitting for my wedding gown.* As often happens with Southern thunderstorms, the rain slacked off into a drizzle and as the clouds parted for the sun, a rainbow appeared. *Okay, that's better.*

Her mother came out onto the porch. "Hey, sweetie, are you ready to go? Susan will be here soon."

"I just have to grab my shoes. They're in the bag on the hearth." Callie stood up and turned to go inside. "I'll get something to drink before we go."

Callie's mother followed her into the kitchen, picking up a legal pad full of notes. "I keep going over our list and it looks like everything is in order. As long as your dress is fine, we'll be in good shape."

The attendant at the bridal shop held the wedding dress unzipped, opened wide and gently folded to the floor so she could step into the satiny white gown with its lace overlay. The sweetheart neckline would lay flat along her chest when the dress they zipped it. *The pearls Aunt Sally gave me are exactly the right length and the double pearl earrings that go with it are perfect. Such a nice gift for my something old.* "You'll want to be sure to put the gown on this way. Then on your wedding day, you won't mess up your hair or wrinkle your dress."

Callie giggled as another attendant steadied her when she wobbled as she carefully put a foot into the opening and then slowly lifted her other leg before settling with both feet inside the dress. "Now I know why you have bridesmaids. And I'm doubly glad I didn't get a poofy ball gown." Deftly, the ladies zipped Callie's gown and stood back so she could see herself in the large floor-to-ceiling mirrors.

The dress fit perfectly. Tentatively, Callie fingered the lace on the bodice. The A-line satin dress with its lace overlay fell smoothly from her bust and over her slender hips. "I'm glad I decided on the lacy three-quarter length sleeves for my gown," Callie said as one of the attendants handed her a pair of gloves. "I really didn't want to deal with long gloves and all those buttons. "My mom and maid of honor are waiting for me. Can I step out and let them see the dress? I think it fits perfectly."

"I agree. Certainly. Let's add your veil. I can just pin the pillbox hat temporarily. Now, let me get the curtains for you. Remember small steps." The attendant smiled as she held back the curtain dividing the fitting room from the showroom and her partner preceded Callie.

Callie's mother was speechless. She smiled, and tears of joy filled her eyes. After just a few seconds she found her voice. "Sweetheart, you look like something from a magazine." Callie made a slow turn to show off the dress.

"You were so right about the lace sleeves and the fingertip-length veil. Joe will absolutely go out of his mind when he sees you," Susan said. "You're gorgeous."

Callie walked around a little more, checking out her reflection in the nearby mirrors, enjoying the admiring looks of other shoppers and sales people. *We did finally settle on the perfect dress. I can't believe this is really happening. In two weeks, I'll be Mrs. Joesph Stevens.*

She turned to go back to the fitting room and her mother reminded her of their plan to go out to lunch in the Thalheimers Tea Room after she changed. "Oh, okay. It shouldn't take too long for me to change and for them to get everything bagged up," Callie said over her shoulder.

All three women were in good spirits as they carefully loaded the wedding dress, cossetted in its garment bag, into the back of her mother's sedan, along with the veil and gloves. "The way they put the gown in the bag made it easier to carry around than I thought it would be. I was so worried about getting it dirty or something," Callie said turning to look at Susan in the back seat. Susan had taken it upon herself as maid of honor to make sure the dress remained stretched out across the seat.

"That's for sure. I'm glad to know we can set an iron to steam if there are some wrinkles." Susan held on to the edge of the garment bag. "We have to remember to take an iron to the church."

"Good idea," Callie said. "I wouldn't have thought of that."

At a red light, Callie's mother looked at her daughter. "You did choose the perfect dress for you, Callie. Although, I'm partial to the ballgown style."

Callie closed her eyes tightly for a moment remembering the arguments she had with her mother about the wedding gown. *I'm just not the princess type. Anyway she finally gave up trying to change my mind.* "Thanks, Momma. Oh, we're already at Thalheimers. I'm not really hungry. I think I just might have hot tea and a popover."

Callie loved having lunch in the Tea Room, especially when they could get one of the round booths that made her feel like she was sitting in an upholstered armchair. It always made her think of the setting in some of the English novels she read. Once they placed their orders, her mother pulled out her legal pad with notes.

"Let me see now. We've got all of our outfits, and the men just need to pick up their tuxedos on the Friday morning before the wedding. Joe's best man should be doing that." Callie's mother paused as she squinted and dug around in her purse. "Ah, here are my reading glasses." She went back to looking over the list.

"Well, I do know tonight your shower is at seven. I've got everything for that," Susan said. "But I'll have to set up the food and decorations when I get home."

"That's wonderful, Susan," Callie said before turning to her mother. "Momma, when will they deliver the flowers for the church and fellowship hall?"

Her mother flipped through the legal pad before answering. "The florist will deliver flowers at nine. Miss Ellen's people will set up the fellowship hall once we're in rehearsal and come back Saturday morning to manage the flowers. Then there's the rehearsal dinner in the Jefferson Hotel dining room at seven. Joe's parents chose a great restaurant."

"Man, Friday will be really busy." Callie tucked her hair behind her ears. *Then we have to be at the salon at eight thirty in the morning.*

Susan took a sip of iced tea and looked at Callie. "The Jefferson restaurant is super." There was a lull in conversation as they thought about how hectic the last couple of weeks before the wedding would be when Susan continued abruptly. "Where did you and Joe decide to go for your honeymoon?"

Callie looked down at the last bit of her popover before answering, knowing her mother wouldn't be happy with their decision. "We're going to spend our wedding night at Aunt Sally's house on Caines Island instead of going anywhere fancy." Callie grinned at her mother and Susan. "It'll be a bit rustic since we haven't been able to go back since the funeral, but that's okay. I'll pick up some food to take with us."

"Oh, Callie." Her mother frowned slightly as she set down her fork. "I so hoped you two would treat yourselves a little bit."

"I know, Momma. You and Dad have been so great paying for most of the wedding, but we decided this is what we really want to do. And besides, we have to be in Charleston Monday morning for Joe to get back to work."

After making sure no one needed anything, their waitress left the check on the table.

"I guess you do have to be practical," her mother said. Looking over the check, she slipped a tip under the edge of her plate. "Are you two ready to go?"

Callie and Susan nodded and began gathering their purses while her mother went to the cashier's counter. Tired, everyone was quiet while walking out to the car. When her mother parked in their driveway, Callie turned to Susan in the back seat. "Want to come in for something to drink before you go home? I'll come around and get my dress from the other side."

"No, I'd better go home so I can make sure everything is ready for this evening," Susan said opening the car door. "Are you sure you can get the dress by yourself?"

"I've got it, and Momma will get the door for me." Callie smiled at her mother and turned to look back at her friend. "Susan, thanks so much for all your help. You're the best maid of honor, ever." Callie blew a kiss to her friend.

"Don't mention it," Susan said as she turned away to go to her car. "I'll see you later tonight."

With her mother's help, Callie got her dress out of the car and into her bedroom. Her mother came in with a step stool so she could hang it from the hook in the ceiling her dad had placed there. "Let's get it out of the garment bag so it won't crease," her mother said. "We'll just keep your door closed so no one sees it before Saturday."

"Okay, Momma, but what if I just drape a sheet around it? It does get stuffy in my room, you know." Callie got down from the step stool and stood staring at her wedding gown. *It's so beautiful. I can't believe Joe and I will be married in just eight days.*

"Well, that would work. I'll get a clothespin while you get the sheet."

Back in Callie's bedroom, her mother unfolded the sheet and handed it up to her daughter. Carefully Callie wrapped the dress. "Is everything hidden, Momma?"

"Yes, here's the clothespin." With the sheet secured over the dress, Callie stepped down, folded the step stool, and leaned it against her bed. "Momma, thank you so much. I'd never have gotten everything together without your help." Callie hugged her mother tightly.

"Ah, Callie, I've had so much fun planning this with you." Her mother released her and took a few steps backward. "Your dad and I got married at the courthouse in Charleston with Sally and Claude as witnesses, you know. So this has been a treat for me, too."

Callie pulled the sash of her bathrobe tighter and sat down on the porch swing as a Carolina wren landed on the porch railing. His throat throbbed as he trilled his morning song. The sun dawned on a cloudless day. *Today I become Mrs. Joseph Stevens. No more little girl. I'm thrilled the day is finally here. I'll miss seeing Momma and Dad every day and knowing where everything is in town, but there's so much waiting for Joe and me.* Hearing her mother at the screen door, Callie got up from the swing, startling the Carolina wren who flew off to the nearby pines.

"I'm coming, Momma." Callie was at the screen door before her mother called her name.

"You should eat, sweetie." Her mother opened the screen door. "Let me make you some scrambled eggs and toast. Or would you rather have over medium?"

"I guess I should eat something. Just scrambled, please." Callie pushed her hair back from her face. "I'm not sure how much I could eat right now; my stomach's doing back flips." Callie grimaced pressing her hands across her middle.

"I'll fix it while you get changed." Her mother hugged her briefly. "It's normal to be a little nervous. You're the star of the show today and you're beautiful. But you need to eat so you don't faint later."

"Okay, Momma, I'll try. I'll be right out since for now, I'm just wearing jeans." As Callie closed her bedroom door, she heard her dad walking down the hall. *Probably going to the kitchen for coffee.*

She returned to the kitchen just as her mother put a plate at her place at the table. After she had settled in her seat her father smiled and squeezed her shoulder for a moment. Abruptly he ran a hand over his eyes, wiping away the tears.

"Ah, Dad, you know I'll always be your little girl," Callie said with a small smile.

"I know, but it seems just yesterday I was teaching you to ride a bike, and today you're getting married," her dad cleared his throat as her mother put a plate of eggs and toast in front of him.

"Okay, you two. Eat up before everything's cold," her mother joined them at the table." Her eyes glittered as she held back tears. "This is supposed to be a happy day for Callie."

"It is. She's definitely made a good choice. By the way, when can I take Callie's things to the church?" Her dad asked as he spread jam on his toast.

"Anytime, now." Her mother put her fork down. "The church is open. Callie, do you have everything ready?"

"Yes, ma'am. My suitcase and overnight bag are packed. And everything else is in the two garment bags." Callie excused herself and stood up. "I'm ready to go to the salon whenever we clean the kitchen."

"Don't worry about that now. Just rinse them and leave the dishes in the sink. Today they can wait," her mother said as she too got up from the table. "Bob, we're taking off now. Guess we'll see you at the church." She kissed her husband on the cheek before going into the living room.

Putting their dishes in the sink, Callie joined her mother. "Just a minute, Momma." Callie hurried back to the kitchen to hug her dad. "Love you, Dad. You're the best dad ever," she said. "I'd better go now before I start blubbering." Callie hurried to join her mother on the porch.

Usually impatient with hair stylists, Callie found herself relaxing while everyone worked to pamper her and get her ready for the ceremony. Within a few hours, her hair was secured in a partial updo that left enough hair down so it could swing to her shoulders without hiding her face. Her nails were manicured and her makeup done. *Well, everyone did a good job. My face still looks like me. Of course, tomorrow I'll probably wreck these nails and it will take a week to get all the hairspray out of my hair.* Callie smiled softly. *Not really my thing, but it seemed to be important to Momma. And she and Susan seem to be enjoying themselves. Momma's worked so hard to make everything perfect for today.*

At the church, her mother and Susan managed to help each other into their gowns before turning their attention to Callie. With their help, Callie slipped into her wedding dress without destroying her hair. After they settled her veil and the pillbox hat, her mother left to take her place in the pews. Callie asked Susan to get her dad. When Callie's dad stepped into the dressing room and stopped within arm's reach of his daughter, Susan stepped out of the room. "Callie-girl, you're---" her dad hesitated and he fished a handkerchief from the inside breast pocket of his tuxedo and dabbed at his eyes. "You're stunning."

"Aw, Dad, thank you." Callie blinked rapidly trying to keep from crying. "I knew we would cry when you first saw me in the dress. So I thought we should have a moment, and then I could say thanks for everything - for teaching me how to fix things around the house, how to play softball, and to love baseball."

Her dad smiled through his tears. "Loved every minute of it. Couldn't have asked for a better daughter." Clearing his throat, drying his tears once more and putting away the handkerchief, he continued. "Are you ready? Shall we go out?"

Taking his offered arm, Callie began her walk down the aisle. She marveled at all the people gathered to celebrate her and Joe's marriage. At the altar she took Joe's hands as her father stepped away. It was clear from the couple's ardent expressions; they were deeply in love.

11

Caines Island/Charleston
September 1965

It was nearly dark when the newlyweds pulled into the driveway on Caines Island. Joe's serious tone made Callie stop on her way to the back of the truck. "What's up?"

"Mrs. Stevens, what are you doing?" Joe frowned with mock seriousness and he walked around to where she stood.

"Well, I thought I would help get our things up to the house, Mr. Stevens," Callie said giggling while Joe reached for her hand.

"That stuff can wait. For now, let me escort you to our honeymoon suite." Joe grinned. Together they walked across the yard and onto the porch. When they reached the door, he motioned for Callie to wait while he unlocked it. Pushing the door open, Joe returned to her side and swept her into his arms. Laughing, Callie buried her head in his shoulder for a moment. "Sorry, I just didn't expect this." When he crossed the threshold, Callie slid from his arms, looked into his eyes as he murmured, "I love you, Callie."

Sunlight filtered through the curtains. Callie quietly slipped out of bed, pulled on the shirt and jeans she wore on the drive yesterday, and slipped into her Keds. *Joe, my love, you get some rest.*

Passing through the living room to the kitchen, she saw the fresh black-eyed susans on the coffee table that she hadn't noticed the night before. *Must have been Alma and Louise. That was so sweet. I did notice they opened up the place and got it ready for us.* Callie rummaged around in the kitchen, looking for the coffee. *Ah, that's right; Aunt Sally always left it in the refrigerator. Joe must have gotten up sometime last night. The food we brought with us is already in here.*

With the coffee brewing, Callie went out to the front porch and settled into a wicker rocking chair. *There's no sound, only the birds and the distant waves. The air is so fresh. Hmm. Coffee must be ready by now.*

Callie returned to the kitchen to see Joe was already pouring coffee. "Good morning my husband." She set milk and sugar on the small, white wooden table with an enameled top. "Did you sleep well?" Callie smiled and sat down.

"Best sleep ever." Joe grinned and placed a mug of coffee in front of her.

Callie blushed. "It was a pretty special night, but we left my gown in the truck."

"Oh? We left your wedding gown with your parents'. Oh, I see, your nightgown." Joe shook his head. "It's okay, I hope. You can wear it tonight. In celebration of our first night in our apartment." He looked at Callie hopefully.

He looks almost sad. "Of course, it will be okay. I'll be sure to wear it tonight."

The newlyweds made plans for the day while sipping coffee. Joe pushed his chair back from the table, "Do you want to shower first? Or should I?"

"You go ahead. I'll start breakfast and shower afterward. But would you bring in the suitcase?"

"Sure, what else needs to come inside?"

"You got our food earlier, so I don't think we need anything else here."

Callie and Joe walked along the beach laughing at the antics of the sandpipers running along the water's edge. "Look at them running from the water and hopping right back to the same place." Joe stopped at the edge of the damp sand, laughing while he watched the birds.

"I know." Callie giggled. "And then there's the seagulls soaring and swooping down like there might be something for them caught in the waves."

Joe pulled her down to the sand and slipped his arm around her waist. Callie rested her head on his shoulder. "Let's sit here a while. You know, this place kinda grows on you."

"Okay, let's just watch the waves and the sandpipers. Guess we can get something at Pete's. I didn't pack anything for lunch."

The sun reached its high point in the sky. Joe shifted in the sand. "I hate to say this, but it's probably noon." He kissed Callie gently on the forehead. "We should get moving."

With a sigh, Callie agreed. "Yeah, let's stop in at Pete's. Alma says he has sandwiches." She stood up and began brushing away the sand from her clothes.

The door chime sounded when they entered the store. "I'll be right there," a voice called from the back. Callie and Joe walked through the aisles grabbing potato chips on their way to the deli counter. A short, rounded man with a gray grizzled beard came through the door to the storeroom and stepped behind the deli counter. "Hi, I'm Pete Jenkins. What can I get for you?" A smile lit up his face.

"Hey, I'm Joe and this is my wife, Callie. We'd like a couple of sandwiches."

"Ah, you're the young folks who inherited Sally's place. I'm sorry about your loss. Sally was a fine person." Pete washed and dried his hands.

"Thank you." Callie lowered her eyes for a moment before looking up and ordering. "I'd like a ham and cheese sandwich."

"I'd like a roast beef sandwich with mayo," Joe said turning to look around the store. "You've got a nice place here."

"Why thank you. My wife, Lyla, and I run the place." Pete kept up a line of chatter as he made Callie's sandwich. "Lydia's in the back baking.

We generally have some type of pastries to go with the coffee. Do you want lettuce and tomato on those sandwiches?"

"Yes, please, on both of them. I see Alma was right. You really are a grocery store." Callie took her sandwich and watched Pete while he deftly made Joe's sandwich.

"Here you go." Pete passed the sandwich to Joe. After washing his hands, he came around the counter. "How long are you here?"

They followed him to the register near the front of the store. "We got in last night, but have to go on to Charleston in a couple of hours." Joe pulled his wallet from his pocket and paid for their purchases.

"Oh, right." Pete tapped his head. "It was your wedding that Max, Louise, and Alma went to in Columbia. Congratulations."

"Thank you," Callie said and took the bag Pete held out to her.

"I'm sure we'll see you next time we're on the island," Joe said as the couple made their way to the door.

"Thank you." Pete turned to go back to the storeroom. "See you next time."

"I think you'll like Anita and Steve. They have the apartment next to us." Joe unlocked the apartment. "Welcome home, honey. I'll take these suitcases into the bedroom."

"I can help once I go to the bathroom." Callie hurried past him. "Leave the presents in the living room. We can open some of them before supper."

With the truck unloaded, they sat on the couch ready to open presents. "Oh, wait a minute. I've got to get some paper and a pen." Callie stood, swiveling her head while she tried to remember where she put her purse. "Oh, there it is, on top of that box by the window." Pulling out her small notepad and a pen, she settled next to Joe on the couch. "Now, I'm ready." Joe unwrapped a box and showed Callie the glasses nestled inside.

"Oh my, these glasses are so pretty. They look almost like sea glass, kinda blue green." Callie held the glass up to the light. "Now, who gave those to us?"

"Mm, let me look at the card again," Joe hunted through the paper. "It was Max and Louise. I'll make a stack of the cards here on the coffee table."

"Okay, I've got it. What's next?" Callie looked up from her paper.

"Oh, this is heavy." Pulling at the wrapping paper, Joe smiled. "I think these are the mixing bowls you wanted. They're from Susan and Bobby."

"They're so pretty. I know I'll use these a lot. Oh, what's that odd-shaped gift?" Callie pointed to a roughly oval shape near the far end of the coffee table.

"It's kinda light to be so big." Joe began unwrapping the present. "A laundry basket with dishcloths and towels. Oh, there's a tag that says, 'Hand woven by Alma."

Callie reached out for the basket. Turning it around in her lap, she said, "Wow. That's so sweet of her. I hear these seagrass baskets last for years and years."

Callie dutifully made another entry on her notepad. By the time they finished opening gifts, the couple realized they had most things they needed to set up housekeeping. "We're really lucky to have such generous family and friends. With our gifts, the things from Aunt Sally, and my hope chest, there's not much we'll have to buy."

"That's super. They've given us a great start. Do you want to save this paper?" Joe looked at the wrapping paper he had folded and placed in a neat stack.

"Let's keep it for now." Callie looked around the cluttered room. "Ah, here we go. I'll take the placemats Momma made for us out of this box, and it can go in here." She passed the box to Joe.

"I'll gather the empty boxes and put them in the back of the truck. We only have two metal trash cans out back, so I'll throw these away at work."

Joe began flattening boxes, while Callie began straightening up the living room and organizing the gifts until she could put things away. *I'll be busy unpacking and cleaning for a week.*

"Honey, are you hungry? I took out some chicken. It should be thawed by now." Callie slipped her hair into a ponytail as she walked toward the kitchen.

"Are you going to fry it?" Joe looked up from the box he was folding, his eyes widening expectantly.

"Yeah, fried chicken, rice, green beans, and biscuits." Callie smiled knowing how much Joe liked her fried chicken. "There should be plenty for you to take for lunch tomorrow."

"Cook anytime you're ready, honey. I'll take this stuff to the truck and be right back."

Callie scooted past Joe when they got into the kitchen. "I'll grab the back door, figure out where everything is, and start supper."

Well, Joe didn't do much cooking in here while I was in Columbia. The cast iron skillet is clean and there's one pot in the cabinet. Callie started digging through a box under the kitchen window. *Ah, that'll do for rice if I can find the lid. Here it is.*

Joe paused in the doorway between the kitchen and the living room. "Should I put the kitchen things with the other boxes under the window?"

"Sounds good. We might have to move the table to make more room. I'm glad you were able to get the furniture from Aunt Sally in here. Good of your friends to help you move everything from your parents' barn."

"Honey, I'm not sure how we got it all in this apartment." Joe shook his head and started moving boxes.

"I know it seems crowded right now, but I'll work on getting things arranged better." *This little four-burner stove sure is different than cooking at Momma's. It'll take some getting used to.*

"Well, we'll have to see." Joe continued trying to put away the gifts they just opened.

Callie started the rice on a back burner, poured oil into the cast iron skillet, and turned on the burner to let the oil get hot. *Not much room on this stove. The green beans will have to simmer up front. The skillet takes up so much room.* When the oil was hot enough, Callie added the flour-coated chicken to the skillet and then moved over to the counter to mix biscuit dough.

"I think I've got things sorted for you. At least the kitchen stuff." Joe wrapped his arms around Callie. "You're making biscuits, too?"

Settling into his embrace, Callie chuckled and said, "You've got to have something besides chicken in that lunch box tomorrow."

After supper, Callie washed dishes while Joe dried them. "It's going to be weird not having a garden to cook from." Callie turned to look at Joe.

"As good as you cook, I don't care where you get it." He playfully poked her in the ribs.

"Well, fresh is better. Maybe I can find a grocery store with good produce." Callie let the water run out and rinsed the sink. "That's that. Let's go watch some TV."

After Joe left for work on Monday, Callie started unpacking in earnest. With a lot of tugging, pushing and pulling, she managed to fit the hutch between the two tall windows in the living room. She placed the table from Aunt Sally's house in Columbia just in front of the hutch. *It'll be a little tight if someone's sitting on that side, but I don't think we'll have that many guests and we can still get in the front door to the right of the windows.* Next, she put the placemats her mother made for them on the table. The predominately green print went well with the avocado green curtains she made in Columbia before the wedding.

She put their television on a small table in front the coal fireplace set in the wall between the kitchen and the living room. The pale green tiles of its surround and hearth cleaned up nicely with some Windex. She managed to move the burnt orange couch over against the opposite wall from the television. *Now this will be a comfy place in the evening.* Turning to look at the whole room, Callie realized there were still two armchairs along with a table and a lamp. *Okay, they'll go along the other wall.*

With the living room settled, Callie made herself a pimento cheese sandwich before she began unpacking boxes holding kitchen items and washing everything before putting them away. The small galley kitchen didn't have much storage space so she put a lot of things in the hutch's lower cabinet.

Finally, she shifted the small table and two chairs that had been on Aunt Sally's back porch in Columbia into place by the kitchen window. *This will be nice for a quick cup of coffee.* Then she sorted the various linens that would need to go to the laundromat into empty boxes. *Time for a break before I start supper. Joe was right, there's not much room in here with the table and hutch.* Callie smiled to herself. *Tomorrow, I'll get the bedroom. That will be much easier since I just have to get our clothes put away.*

Supper was almost ready when Joe got home from work. "Honey, we can actually move in here," Joe smiled as he walked through the kitchen and into the living room before stopping to give Callie a quick kiss. "I'd give you a hug, but I'm dirty and sweaty."

"It's okay, honey. So am I." Callie wrapped her arms around him. "You've got time for a shower before dinner's ready."

Several minutes later, Joe came into the kitchen drying his hair with a towel. "Hmm. Smells good in here." He draped the towel around his neck. "Anything I can do to help?"

"You can set the table. " Joe looked questioningly at the kitchen table. "The one in the other room, while I get things into bowls," Callie said.

"Okay, do you want iced tea with supper? And where are the plates?" Joe laughed as Callie swatted him with a kitchen towel.

"Same place they were last night, silly." Callie kept laughing as she spooned the mashed potatoes into a bowl. Just hamburger steaks for dinner tonight, but there's gravy to go with it." Callie took the mashed potatoes to the table along with the meat and gravy before going back to get the lima beans.

Joe placed their drinks on the table before sitting down. "Honey, it really looks nice in here. Like a home."

Callie sat beside him at the table. "Thanks, it took a while to get this room and the kitchen done, but tomorrow I should be able to get the bedroom."

The couple was quiet for a few minutes as they ate. "Do you think I could drive you in on Thursday?" Callie looked at Joe expectantly.

"Sure. What's up." Joe put his fork on his plate.

"There's a lot of laundry to do. And the laundromat will be packed on Saturday from what Anna said to me when I saw her on the porch." Callie picked up her biscuit and put some peach jam on it. "If I get done early enough, I can do the grocery shopping, too."

"Yeah, honey. Glad you're meeting some of the neighbors. Let me have some of that jam." Joe slathered jam on his biscuit and inhaled it in just a few bites. "Man, I'm stuffed."

"I'll just get the kitchen cleaned up and then we can watch some TV."

As Callie began clearing the table, Joe stood up. "I'll bring everything in to you. I'm pretty beat but after I put my feet up a bit, I'll come in and dry."

After the couple settled into their apartment, Callie found a job at a diner in downtown Charleston that catered to local businessmen. She only worked the lunch shift, and with her hours so different from Joe's, she rode the bus to and from work. Today she planned to pick up a few groceries on her way home. Joe had been talking about having country fried steak and it had been a while since she had served it for supper.

I'll have to get off the bus near the Piggly Wiggly. Maybe I'll find a special or something. We've got the electrician looking at the wiring in Aunt Sally's place this week, and we want to do some painting there. I can't wait to get home and let my hair down. Callie rubbed her temples. *I get why we have to wear it up, but this bun gives me a headache.*

12

Caines Island 1970

Callie pulled her hair back into a ponytail before settling Kimberly in her sling. "How's Momma's baby girl? Ready to go for a walk?" Kimberly smiled and waved her arms randomly. Approaching the tidal pools dotted with blue-gray herons, she took deep breaths of the salty air. *Such tall stately birds. Oh, we're at the dunes already.* Yellow-gold sea oats danced in the wind. The sound of waves crashing on the shore had a steady rhythm that Callie found comforting.

"Kimberly, we're going to stay here. I haven't figured out how yet, but I'll find a way. I know Grandma wants us to go to Columbia. Look at those sandpipers scrambling at the edge of the water. Can't wait for you to actually be able to see them. They were your Daddy's favorite island bird."

The infant whimpered and wiggled in the sling. Callie lifted the sling's flap, designed to block the sun, and looked at her daughter. Kimberly was sucking on the back of her hand and looking a little pink. "Are you hungry, sweetie? It got hot quick. We'll go home now."

At home, Callie removed the baby's clothes, except for a sleeveless t-shirt and her diaper, and patted her skin with a damp cloth. The ceiling fan whirled softly creating a light breeze. "Sorry, baby. I forgot how warm you get in the sling. I'll be sure to walk early in the morning from now on." Kimberly began to fuss more intently.

"I know, I know. You're hungry too. Let me sit down in the rocking chair." Kimberly nuzzled Callie's chest. "Here you go, here you go." Callie wrinkled her nose when Kimberly latched on to her breast and then smiled with relief as she felt the release of her breastmilk. Several minutes passed before Kimberly's eyes fluttered and she drifted off to sleep. *You do eat well, and the doctor says you're healthy. I just worry about doing the right thing.*

Callie settled her daughter in the crib and went to change her top which had become damp with sweat from her walk on the beach. *I can't believe I let Kimberly get so hot. I should have known better.* A knock at the front door interrupted Callie's thoughts.

Callie opened the door. "Oh, hi Brenda. Come on in. Kimberly's asleep, but we can talk in the kitchen." Looking at the truck in the driveway, she added. "Is that Josie with you?"

Brenda stepped into the living room. "Yeah, we wanted to drop this off and let you know we were going to town."

"Kimberly's sleeping so I can't go with you today. How about a glass of iced tea before you go?" Callie stepped onto the porch and waved for Josie to join them inside.

The three women gathered in the kitchen. Callie took out glasses and opened the refrigerator to get out the tea.

"Sorry you can't go with us today. It'd do you good to get out for a while," Brenda handed Callie the platter. "This is just some roast, potatoes, and carrots."

"Thanks so much." Callie put the platter in the refrigerator and poured the tea. "You guys have been such a great help, hanging out here with me, but I really don't feel up to going anywhere, even if Kimberly was awake." Callie brought the glasses to the table, pulled out a chair, and joined her friends.

"Honey, it's going to take time---" Josie reached out and squeezed Callie's hand briefly.

"I just can't seem to think straight. Earlier I was walking with Kimberly in her sling, and I let her get overheated." Callie hid her face in her hands. "I just don't know."

Brenda got up from the table, knelt beside Callie, and put an arm around her waist. "Kimberly's fine, isn't she? No way she'd get sunburned in that sling of yours. When's the last time you had a good night's sleep?"

Callie looked at her with tear-filled eyes and shrugged. "Yeah, she's fine. I don't really seem to sleep much."

"All you need is some rest, Callie," Josie said gently. "Does Kimberly ever take formula, or do you have some breast milk in the refrigerator?"

"Yeah, I've got some frozen." Callie's brow puckered, not sure what her friend was suggesting.

Brenda stood up and looked at Josie thoughtfully. "Josie, I only need a couple of things in town. Could you pick them up for me?" Josie nodded. "Okay, Callie. Take out enough milk for Kimberly's next feeding and go rest."

"But your boys..." Callie started before Josie cut her off.

"If Brenda's not home when the bus comes, I'll get them. We're just grilling outside today, and we'll have plenty for everyone." Josie stood and picked up her purse. "I'll check in when I'm back from town."

Callie got up from the table and Brenda followed her to look in the kitchen cabinets. "All right since you insist. Let me show you where things are in the kitchen."

Within a few minutes, Callie had Brenda set up to feed Kimberly. "When she wakes up, I usually change her and then feed her. Everything is either in the dresser or her closet. Make yourself lunch if you get hungry."

"I will," Brenda assured her.

Callie walked down the hallway to the bedroom and softly closed the door. *I don't know the last time I had a good sleep.* Slipping her jeans off, Callie got into bed and pulled the cover over her. *There's so much I need to figure out. Maybe they're right. If I rest maybe I'll be able to think straight. I can't keep just drifting through the days like this.*

13

Caines Island 1967

Callie settled in the wicker rocking chair on the front porch while she took a break from painting and waited for Joe to get back from the lumber yard in Mount Pleasant. Since they hadn't been sure of the weather last night, he decided to pick up the lumber this morning while she painted.

It is so quiet. Charleston has so much hustle and bustle, even in the neighborhoods. So many people. She took a deep breath and let it out slowly. *I can hear the tide coming in even if I can't see the ocean through the trees. That magnolia will smell so good in the summer. Once we're in the house I'll redo these chairs. We're so lucky. Aunt Sally left so many things here. I like things that people used and held in their hands. When I touch them it's like a deeper connection to them somehow.*

Joe pulled into the driveway. She slipped her ball cap on and went to meet him. He already had the tailgate down when Callie got to the truck, and she began to pull several boards toward herself.

"Hold on a minute. You want to lead, or should I?" Joe paused before lifting the end of the stack of lumber from the truck's tailgate.

"You lead. You know where you want to work with this." Callie rested the lumber against her hip while Joe settled his end.

"Okay, let's go to the backyard. I probably could have gotten closer, but we don't have any gravel closer to the house and I don't want to drive through what grass we have there. Ready to go?" Joe looked back to be sure Callie was ready.

Callie smiled and nodded. "Go ahead. I'm fine."

They walked around to the backyard. "All right, let's put it down here next to the sawhorses." Joe put his end down across one of the blocks he set up to keep the lumber off the ground. "Go ahead set your end down."

With the lumber resting on the blocks, Callie took off her ball cap, ran her fingers through her damp hair, and wiped the sweat from her forehead with her sleeve. "I don't know how you work in this heat all day." Settling her cap back on her head, she said, "We've got two more bundles to bring back here, right?"

"Yeah, if you're up to it," Joe grinned at Callie. "I could get it myself."

"No, I'm fine. Two of us can carry more at a time so you can get to framing out the laundry room after lunch. Let's go." She turned and went back around to the truck.

Now that they had a system, moving the lumber went more quickly and Callie went inside to get lunch ready. "It won't take but a few minutes to get things set out. I brought some potato salad, sliced tomatoes, and chicken left from last night's supper."

Joe followed her into the house. "I'll just double-check a few things, and then I'll be there to eat."

With everything out on the table, they sat down. "So tell me again about the laundry room. Is it going to be like a closet?" Callie asked while she fixed her plate.

"Yeah, kinda. You'll have a shelf over the washer and where the dryer will go when we get one. And there'll be enough room for you to put the laundry basket between them." Joe turned in his chair to look at the space where the laundry room was going to be. "I think I can get some rods for hanging stuff up."

"That'll be cool. It'll be nice to have it right here. And not everything goes in the dryer." Callie smiled and went back to eating. "I do like the idea of the bifold doors so I can get to everything."

Joe looked thoughtful for a moment. "What would you think if I built a cabinet for a fold-out ironing board?"

"That's a cool idea. But I don't iron that much though. Not like our mommas did." She picked up her chicken and paused. "As long as there's space where I can store it in the laundry room, that'd be fine."

"Okay. I saw plans for one in my *Handyman's* magazine. Just trying to make things easier for you." Joe smiled and winked at her.

Callie grinned back. "Thanks, honey, but having the laundry room right here in the kitchen is great. It'll be so much nicer than going to the laundromat." Pushing her chair back from the table, she asked. "Have you had enough to eat? I've got some pimento cheese in the fridge."

Joe got up from the table. "I've had plenty." He gave Callie a hug. "When are we supposed to go to Max and Louise's?

"We should be there about five-thirty. Alma is going to ride with us. I don't know about Brenda's or Josie's family." Callie began clearing the table. "After I finish cleaning up after lunch, I'll paint our bedroom with that mold and mildew prevention stuff. Unless you need me here?"

Joe stopped at the back door before stepping onto the porch, "No, just keep doing what you're doing. If I need a hand, I'll holler."

Callie wandered into the kitchen when she finished painting and found Joe nailing the baseboard in the laundry room. "I've stopped painting for now. I'll go ahead and get a shower. Hey, this really looks good."

Joe stood up and stretched. "Thanks. A shower sounds good. You'll be able to paint here tomorrow before we go home. Let me know when you're out." Joe kissed Callie lightly before going out onto the porch.

Pulling on a robe after her shower and wrapping her hair in a towel, Callie stepped to the screen door to let Joe know she was finished. She was back in the bedroom digging in their suitcase when Joe came in. *It's too hot for jeans. Where are those shorts, I packed? Ah, here they are.* Combing out her mass of long, dark brown hair, Callie decided it was too hot to wear it down so she braided it and wrapped it around her head like a crown before going to the kitchen to shuck the corn they were taking to the cookout.

Joe had just finished his shower and made it into the bedroom when Alma walked onto the back porch. “Hey there, Callie. Am I too early?” Alma opened the screen door and stepped into the kitchen.

“No. Joe’s nearly ready. Would you like something to drink? I’ve got fresh iced tea.”

Callie stood up from the kitchen table.

“No thanks. I wanted to bring you a few eggs. The peach pie is for tonight.” Alma set the brown bag with eggs and pie on the table and pivoted to look at the kitchen. “You guys are moving right along.” She grinned and nodded approvingly.

“Thanks. We’ve been working at a pretty good pace. We did take time for an early morning walk on the beach.” Callie put the eggs in the refrigerator. “And thanks for the eggs. When we’re here full time, I’ll have a vegetable garden and I’ll share with you from that.” Callie grinned. “I can hardly wait. Momma always had a vegetable garden and we canned.” She shook her head and laughed. “I’ve never eaten so many store bought vegetables in my life.”

Alma laughed along with her and said, “I don’t can much with just myself to cook for, but I do put up stuff in the freezer.”

Callie checked to see that she had corn holders to go with the fresh corn she would boil once they were at Max and Louise’s. As she closed up the bag, Joe came into the kitchen. “Hey, Miss Alma. So good to see you.” He gave Alma a hug before turning to Callie. “Are we ready, honey?” Callie nodded. “Okay, let’s go relax for a while.”

Callie scooted to the middle of the truck’s seat. “We could almost walk to Max and Louise’s if we didn’t have this stuff to carry.”

“Remind me to show you the path that cuts through this loop in the road.” Alma settled the pie on her lap before continuing. “It goes through the roads’ right of way. We’ve used it for so many years that it’s a nice wide path. Max and Steve always keep the bushes back.

Joe glanced briefly at Alma. "I'll help keep it cut back, too. Oh, we're here already. Hold on, let me help with that pie, Alma." Joe parked the truck under the shade of an oak tree and hurried around the truck to take the pie.

Two trestle-style picnic tables covered with bright tablecloths sat under the shade of the live oaks in Max and Louise's front yard. Spanish moss hanging from their branches fluttered in the breeze. There was a third table nearby with pitchers of iced tea, lemonade, a stack of plates, and a basket of silverware. "Hey, good to see you guys," Louise called as she glided across the yard like a dancer. "Alma, just leave the pie on that table with the drinks."

Max turned from the grill to wave at everyone. "Come on Callie, the pots are boiling. Let's get the corn started then I can start the shrimp. Josie and Brenda, with their families, should get here soon."

Brenda, along with her husband and their two sons, were the next to arrive. Josie and her family pulled into the driveway right behind them.

"Hiya, guys. Good to see you," Callie said. "Does anybody need a hand?"

Josie stood next to her car. "Could you come get this banana pudding? I've got to get the watermelon while my guys get a few extra chairs."

Hearing Josie, Joe went to help unload chairs while Callie got the pudding. As she passed Brenda on the way back to the tables, she asked. "Are you okay? Do you need any help?"

"No, we've got this." Brenda turned to her oldest son, reminding him to get the basket of rolls.

Once they deposited their items near the picnic tables, the children started a game of tag. Their peals of laughter brought smiles to the adults' faces as they began putting out the last of the food.

"Come and get it kiddos," Louise called out from under the live oaks. "Supper's on."

Quickly everyone served themselves sides from the buffet table. Bowls of shrimp lined the picnic tables so plates could easily be refilled.

"How's work going on the house?" Max asked when he sat down following grace.

"It's coming along," Joe answered and helped himself to shrimp. "The wiring was updated a couple of weeks ago."

"Well, that's always good." Josie's husband, Tom, put in while he peeled a shrimp. "I don't know that Miss Sally ever had anything like that done."

"Nah, she hadn't. And he put in a 220 outlet for a dryer." Joe turned his attention to his plate.

"When do you think you guys will be here full-time?" Louise looked at Callie, who was buttering an ear of corn.

"We'll have most stuff done in another couple of trips, but we don't want to break our lease. So probably not until next July." Callie shrugged. "I'd really like to put in a vegetable garden, but I'll have to wait a while longer."

"Well, once you're here, you can go to the Tyler's Truck Farm in Mount Pleasant." Alma looked around Tom to see Callie. "They do supply grocery stores, but they have a stand, too. Prices are good enough that you could buy it there and then can it like you were talking about this morning."

"Now that would be great. I'm not used to having to buy canned goods." Callie laughed. "I'm going to get some of that banana pudding. Can I get something for anybody else while I'm there?"

"Honey, would you bring back some for me, too?" Joe began gathering shrimp peels, placing them and his silverware on the plate.

"Sure, anybody else?" Callie got up and made her way to the desserts. There were a few requests for the banana pudding and one of Josie's boys wanted a slice of peach pie. With the requests honored, Callie took her serving and rejoined the adults at the table.

With dessert finished, everyone helped return the yard to some semblance of order. Some carried dishes inside and began washing them. Louise came in and insisted the dishes be left in the drainer since she couldn't get anyone to stop washing. "Just come on outside when you're done."

Josie and Brenda's families were the first to leave since the boys started getting tired and cranky. Joe and Max moved one of the tables back into the large workshop Max had behind the house. "You've got everything in here." Joe took a moment to admire Max's woodworking tools. "I'd like to build a shop one day. There's just a storage shed on the property, now. Not much room to work in there."

"Yeah, know what you mean." Max shook his head. "Claude was a great businessman, but he and Sally weren't very handy." They stepped outside and Max closed up the shop.

"Well, I'll never make money like he did." Joe shrugged his shoulders. "Anyway, I'll eventually get around to building my shop. Right now, we've got to save up. Once we move to the island, Callie'll have to stop working." The two men made their way to the front yard.

Max glanced at Joe. "No, wouldn't pay for her to drive back and forth to that diner." He frowned slightly. "And you just have the truck, right?"

"Yeah, it's starting to cost more in repairs than it's worth. So I'm going to need a work truck. Maybe then we can get her a car." Joe shoved his hands into the pockets of his jeans.

Max clapped him on the back and a wide smile spread across his face. "Few of us can do everything all at once. You and Callie have time to get all that stuff done. You're doing a great job with the house."

Dusk was settling across the yard as the men returned to the picnic tables in the front yard. Callie stifled a yawn and looked across the table at Alma. "Are you ready to go home? I'm pooped and there's more painting for me to get done tomorrow."

"Yeah, I've got to check the chickens before it's full dark." Alma eased herself up and out of her seat. The trio gathered their dishes and traded hugs with Max and Louise before making their way home. Once they dropped Alma off, Joe and Callie made their way through the house and climbed into bed.

Dappled shadows were playing across the bed when Callie woke up. She looked lovingly at Joe lying next to her. *He looks so peaceful. He's got to be tired. I'll let him sleep a little longer. There's a lot to do today before we go back to Charleston.* Slipping out of bed, she quickly pulled on her painting clothes from yesterday and slipped into the pair of Keds she left at the house for days like today. *I'm so messy, no sense ruining another outfit or pair of shoes.*

Softly closing the bedroom door behind her, Callie went into the kitchen and started the coffee. *I'll wait on the porch for that to get ready.* Spanish moss drifted away from the oak trees branches in the early morning breeze. The sun gave the sky a pink tint as it began its trek above the horizon. *Love the smell of salty ocean air.* Herons and seagulls took wing from the marshes just around the bend, filling the sky as they made their way to the ocean. She took a deep breath. *Bet the coffee's ready. After a few sips of that, think I'll paint the laundry room. We'll be able to put it back together before we go.*

Working quickly, Callie was able to get the laundry room painted before Joe got up. "Hey, why'd you let me sleep so long?" Joe groused as he shuffled into the kitchen.

"You did a lot yesterday. You deserved it." Callie pushed a strand of hair back into her ball cap. "The laundry room is painted. I've got to clean up my roller and then I'll start breakfast. What did you want to do today?" Bending over Callie collected her painting supplies and paused by the kitchen table.

"I wanted to make a cover for the deep sink on the porch and hook up the washing machine so we can check the plumbing. Other than that, nothing much. Maybe take a walk and stop in at Pete's before we go home."

"Okay, sounds good. I'll be back inside in a minute. Just enjoy that coffee." Callie smiled as she opened the door to the porch and returned to the kitchen.

While Callie started bacon, Joe slipped the washer into place and turned on the water. "Oh, good. Nice and level. I know there weren't any leaks under the house when I ran the line. So we should be in business." Joe turned on the washing machine to check its hose connections. "Okay, it's good to go. Man, that bacon smells good." Joe crossed the kitchen and wrapped his arms around Callie's waist as she stood in front of the stove.

Callie leaned against him until the bacon grease began popping. Laughing, she stepped out of the embrace. "We're both going to get burned. Get us more coffee. I'll put the eggs on our plates and bring them to the table."

Joe patted her rear playfully and rounded up their coffee mugs. By the time he had them refilled, Callie had their plates on the table. With hearty appetites spurred by fresh air and hard work, it wasn't long before they finished breakfast. "I'll make that cover while you take care of the kitchen. Then we should just be lazy for a while." Joe took his dishes to the counter by the sink.

"Sounds like a good idea. We've both got to work tomorrow." Callie followed him to the sink with her dishes. "I'll get everything ready to close up again while I'm at it."

It wasn't long before Joe finished with the cover for the deep sink on the back porch. Tapping on the kitchen window overlooking the sink, Joe motioned for Callie to come outside. Callie stood in the kitchen doorway.

"I've finished it." Built on casters, it looked like a cabinet when it was in place. He had even put pulls on the false drawer and door on the front.

"Wow, honey. That's really cool. Now the sink won't get all dirty. Glad you didn't listen to me when I wanted to get rid of it because it was ugly with all the dried paint and stuff."

"See if you can pull it out." Joe stood off to the side so Callie could reach the sink.

"Oh, that's easy." Callie pulled the cover out and put it back in place. "I really like this."

Joe grinned. "Okay, I've got to put my tools in the truck, clean up some of these shavings and I'll be through for the day. Do you need my help inside before we go for a walk on the beach?" He began wrapping up the extension cord as he walked to the screen door leading outside.

"No, I've just got to get stuff into the suitcase. Most of it's dirty anyway. I should be done about the same time you are." Callie went back inside anxious to get down to the shore.

14

Caines Island 1968

Callie woke up early and stretched as she got up. She developed the habit when she began working at the diner. Tears gathered in the corners of her eyes as she realized that this was the last time she and Joe would wake up in the Charleston apartment. Their first home as a married couple tugged at her heartstrings for a moment or two. Brushing the tears from her eyes, Callie smiled thinking of their future on the island.

We'd better get up and get moving. Joe's friends from work will be here soon. Callie sat up, leaned over, and brushed her lips against Joe's cheek. "Wake up sleepyhead. The guys'll be here before long." She rolled over to her side of the bed and got up. Still lying on the bed, Joe stretched and yawned. "Okay. I'm getting up. Is there anything that still needs to be packed?" he asked sitting up on the side of the bed.

"No, we used paper plates last night. I've got some Krispy Kreme doughnuts to have with coffee." Callie gathered her nightgown and put it in a laundry basket. "Just throw your pajama bottoms in the basket. Once you're up, I'll strip the bed. Right now, I'll start the coffee."

Joe joined her in the kitchen after his shower. "Thanks for getting my coffee ready. Does it matter what gets taken first?" He sipped his coffee and picked up a doughnut.

"I'll be sure the coffee pot goes with us. Other than that, it doesn't matter. On second thought, I should leave it here until I finish cleaning the apartment." Callie puffed out a breath as a small frown creased her forehead. "How long do you think it'll take to get everything moved?"

Joe rubbed his chin. "Charles and Tim are each driving their trucks. So, we can probably get everything moved today. Do we need anything from the store to feed the guys?"

"No. We've got everything. I started the hamburger thawing last night." She took a bite of her doughnut and washed it down with coffee. "When I finish this. I'll start putting stuff in the cooler. Should I grill tonight, or do you want to?"

"Not sure. Let's see when we get the last load to the house. If it's later, you might have to." Hearing a knock at the front door, Joe went to answer it.

"Hey, Charles, Tim. Come on in." Joe led his friends through the maze of boxes and into the kitchen.

"Hi guys. Would you like a cup of coffee?" Callie offered. "We've got donuts, too." Tim shook his head and looked at the boxes stacked everywhere.

"No, I'm good," Charles said, looking around the apartment. "Where do you want to start, Joe?"

"Let's start with the boxes in the kitchen and the living room." Tim and Charles followed Joe as he left the kitchen. "We can get the furniture on the last run. All the appliances stay with the apartment so there's really nothing heavy to move."

"Good deal," Tim said as he picked up a box. "I say let's get going then. It's going to be a hot one today."

"That's for sure. Let's load your truck first Charles." Joe reached into his pocket for his keys. "I'll move my truck around the front and then help with the loading."

By mid-afternoon, they had transported the maze of boxes to the island house. Most of the boxes were in the spare bedroom Callie wanted to turn into a sewing room when they got things settled. Other boxes went into the rooms they belonged in. After the first trip, Callie stayed behind to unpack.

There won't be a lot of room in here once the bed's up. Never realized how small the two closets are. I'll hang up what I can. The rest will go into the dressers when they get here. The guys should get back soon. I'd better start getting things ready for the burgers.

She was putting the hamburger patties in the refrigerator when she heard the trucks pull into the driveway. On her way to the front porch, Callie propped open the front door and called out, "Hey guys, come get something to drink before you start unloading."

"Thanks honey, but we just want to be done with this; it won't take long to unload." Joe waved, smiled, and walked to the back of the truck.

"Okay, I'll get the charcoal started." Callie walked around to the side porch and out its door where they had the grill set up. After the charcoal began to flame, she covered the grill and then went inside to slice tomatoes and onions for the burgers.

"Callie, those burgers hit the spot." Charles leaned back in his chair.

"Thanks, Charles. Glad you enjoyed it. My neighbor Alma brought over a peach pie. Could I get some for you?" Callie stood up and began gathering empty plates. "How about you, Tim?"

"Hmm, maybe just a little. That potato salad sure was good." Tim stretched in his chair.

Joe got up and began gathering things from the table. "I'll help you, honey."

"Thanks, sweetheart. I've got coffee, too." Callie continued on her way to the kitchen while Joe followed.

Joe served the pie. Callie covered a heavy cookie sheet with a kitchen towel and placed mugs, coffee, milk, and sugar on it before carrying everything outside. After they had eaten dessert, drank all the coffee, and exhausted the topic of baseball, talk turned to prospects for the upcoming football season.

Callie quietly cleared the remnants of dessert from the table and started cleaning up the kitchen. *Well, that went okay. Not that doing a cookout is hard. The apartment was so small that we never had people over to eat. Maybe they can come again and bring their girlfriends.* Dishes were in the drainer when the guys drifted in from the porch.

"Callie, thanks again for cooking," Tim said giving Callie a quick hug. "It was real good."

"No, thank both of you for helping move everything. We'd still be at it if it weren't for you guys." Callie slipped her arm around Joe's waist and looked up at him. "Isn't that right, honey?"

"That's for sure." Joe gave Callie a squeeze. "Charles, I think I've got you blocked in. I'll go move my truck. I'm trying not to tear up what yard we've got." Joe chuckled as he led the way outside.

The sun was well over the horizon by the time Callie made her first cup of coffee the next morning and carried it out to the front porch. Settling into the wicker rocking chair, she took several deep breaths. The vibrant landscape enchanted her as she sipped her coffee. Along the fence line between their yard and Alma's, hydrangea bushes nodded their pink and blue snowball-like blossoms. *Everywhere I look there's beautiful color.* She giggled out loud as she watched a Carolina wren perch on the porch railing seemingly unconcerned by her presence as he flitted down to the floor. The little russet-brown bird with its distinctive white eye shadow cocked his head at her before continuing his search for food as he hopped around. With one last look he flew off to the nearby shrubs. *We did it. We're really living in Aunt Sally's house. It will take me some time to get everything together. I don't know how we managed to get so much stuff in that little apartment.*

Later that morning, Callie sat on the floor to put pots and pans into a lower cabinet. She stood up when she heard Joe behind her. "Good morning, honey. Are you hungry?"

"I'll have some coffee first. Do we have any ham left?" Joe fixed a mug of coffee and sat down at the kitchen table. "Why don't you take a break? Get some coffee. In a bit, I'll make some ham and egg sandwiches before we go back to the apartment."

"That sounds good." Callie refilled her coffee cup and joined Joe at the table. "There isn't much to do at the apartment. I think we can be out of there in a couple of hours."

Joe looked around the kitchen. "I don't think we can fit Aunt Sally's kitchen table from Columbia in here. There's really not enough room for a dining area in the living room either." He turned to look back at Callie.

Callie raised an eyebrow as she thought. "Well, if you can do something to protect the wood, we could use it on the porch." She looked at Joe hopefully.

Laughing, Joe shook his head. "You really can't stand getting rid of anything that's related to family. Can you?" After thinking a little bit, he continued. "Yes, I can do that."

Callie's eyes sparkled as she grinned and gave him a hug. "I just feel a deeper connection when I use old things. It doesn't have to be something big. That's why I've kept so many of Aunt Sally's kitchen utensils." Callie gave a self-deprecating chuckle. "Sounds silly when I say it out loud."

"No, honey." Joe held her close. "Not silly. Just one of the things I love about you." Releasing the embrace, Joe stood up. "Let me make our sandwiches."

"I'll gather up the cleaning supplies while you do that. What do you want for supper?" Callie asked while she put cleaning supplies in a bucket.

"I don't know. I think we should just take it easy when we get back. Maybe spend time on the beach. We can always get something at Pete's." Joe turned back to the stove.

Pausing on her way to the porch, Callie frowned slightly. "I don't mind cooking, you know."

"I know, and you do a good job of it. But this moving has been a lot of work." Joe put a plate at Callie's place at the table. "I think we both deserve a rest. Come eat."

"I'll be right there. Just want to put this bucket on the porch." Within a couple of minutes, Callie sat at the table with Joe. "Well, okay. Guess we could use a rest." She stood up, gathered their dishes before going to the counter. Looking back at Joe, she continued. "Let's get back to the apartment so we can be through with that."

People were leaving the pier as the young couple made their way to the ocean late in the afternoon. A breeze negated part of the sun's warmth. Waves crashed further up the shoreline as high tide approached. Undaunted, sandpipers pursued their meal with a characteristic hop forward and then hop backward approach to avoid the ocean's march along the shoreline.

"These sandpipers beat all I've ever seen. Always the same dance, and unless we get too close, they're just as happy for us to be here." Joe grinned, linking hands with Callie while they walked down the beach.

"I know what you mean. And as soon as the water recedes, they're right back at the same place." Callie brushed her hair away from her face. "Maybe we'll see the herons on our way home. They're so tall and majestic." She sank to the sand, looking out at the white-crested waves making their way to shore.

Sitting down beside her, Joe leaned in to say, "This would be a wonderful place to raise our kids."

Callie wrapped her arms around him. "I think so too. Think I'll stop taking the pill after this round."

Joe held her close. "I was hoping you'd see it that way.

15

" Caines Island 1969

Callie settled into her wicker rocking chair on the front porch and watched Joe's truck pull out of the driveway. The magnolia's sweet, heavy scent permeated the still air. Spanish moss hung limply in the live oak trees. A Carolina wren rested on the porch railing with a bit of dried grass in its beak. *So cool, to watch the birds build their nest. Later, there'll be so many little ones. I wonder if the wren is building her nest near the back porch. Ah, there's Alma.*

Callie waved as she called out to her friend, "Morning, come have some coffee." Alma nodded and waved back. "Be right there."

Callie went inside to fix her friend's coffee and refill her own cup. When she returned, Alma was seated in a rocking chair. "Here you go." Callie handed Alma her coffee and relaxed in a nearby chair. She tried to stifle a yawn without much success and put a hand in front of her mouth. "I'm so tired lately." Her arm bumped against her breast as she lowered it to the chair's armrest. "Ouch."

Alma smiled over her coffee cup. "Hey, are you in the family way?" Her brown nearly black eyes danced and she grinned as she watched Callie frown.

"Well, it's possible. I am a little late, but things have been more irregular since I stopped my birth control pills several months ago." Callie's frown turned into a grin. "I'll make an appointment with Dr.

Reilly as soon as the office opens." Callie took a few even breaths. "I'm trying not to get my hopes up, but we're really ready to start our family. I wonder if there's something special, I should be doing." Her expression was thoughtful.

"You mean if you're expecting?" Alma reached over to pat Callie's arm. "No, sugar. You just keep doing what you regularly do. You eat well enough. Maybe don't go into weightlifting since that's not something you do."

Callie broke out into another grin and looked into her empty coffee cup. "Well, I need to finish planting those beans today." She and Alma went into the house.

"I know you two have your hearts set on starting your family now." Alma hugged her friend. "But just be patient."

Alma turned to leave as Callie rinsed their cups and set them on the counter.

Callie brought two glasses of tea out to the front porch where Joe sat after a long day at work. "Here honey, have some tea." She handed him a glass before she settled next to him on the porch swing. "Supper will be ready in about an hour.

"Thanks, sweetheart." Joe took a long drink. "Good, I'll sit for a little bit before we eat. How was your day?" He started swinging in a lazy, gentle motion.

Callie grinned as she linked her arm in his. "The doctor's office called this afternoon." She paused, watching his face light up with excitement.

"What did they say?" Joe stopped the swing and looked into Callie's face. "Are we parents?"

"Yes." Callie bounced on the swing. "They called early this morning. I have an appointment next Wednesday."

Joe hugged her closely, nearly spilling their drinks. "They're sure? I can't believe it."

"I haven't told anyone else." Callie rested her head on his shoulder. "We can call our parents after supper."

Joe stroked her hair gently. "I'm so excited to be a dad. You'll be the best mom ever. When is the baby due?"

"I'm not sure. I think around the end of August or early September. When I go to the doctor's next week, we'll have a better idea." Callie sat up smiling. "Finish your tea. I've got to start the rice." She stood up and gave him a quick kiss. Joe held onto her hand as she started for the door.

"Do I have time for a shower before supper?" He got up and followed her inside.

"Sure, honey. Take your time."

Callie was setting the table when Joe came back into the kitchen. "I'll get this while you finish up supper. I'm guessing you were waiting for me to get out before you made gravy."

"Nah, everything's ready. You finish up here and I'll put it on the table." Callie made her way to the stove and opened the oven. Looking over her shoulder, she asked. "Do we have enough trivets on the table?"

"There are three here. Do I need to get more?" Joe answered as he went to the refrigerator. "Do you want iced tea?"

"Yes, we need one more. And yes, my glass is here by the stove." She carried the bowls with rice and green beans to the table. "I'll get the roast and the gravy. Then we can eat."

When she returned to the table with the rest of the meal, Joe looked at her quizzically. "When did you start putting food in the oven to keep it warm?"

Callie shrugged her shoulders. "Momma did it all the time, especially during the holidays. I wrap any meat up so it doesn't dry out."

While they ate, the young couple made plans for turning the spare bedroom into a nursery. Joe wanted to buy baby furniture right away, but Callie talked him into waiting at least until after she saw the doctor.

"Well, we could at least reorganize your sewing room so we can put the spare bed in there." Joe squeezed her hand. "I just want to get started. I'm so excited."

"Okay, we can do that much. Then we can see about painting later." Callie squeezed his hand. "I'll want to be able to sew in there pretty quickly so I can make baby clothes when we're sure about the due date and all." Callie's eyes danced as she envisioned caring for their baby.

"I guess waiting to buy stuff makes some sense." Joe turned his palms up in surrender. "I just want to have everything ready when the baby gets here."

"Me too," Callie said as she stood up from the table. "Let me get the kitchen cleaned up and we can call our parents."

Joe stood up and began gathering plates. "I'll dry if you wash." Within a short time, they finished the dishes.

Both sets of grandparents were ecstatic to hear the news. Callie's mother let them know she had kept a few of Callie's baby things and that she looked forward to helping get the nursery ready. They were planning to visit in a couple of weeks. Joe's parents were coming at the end of the month.

Sunlight filtering through their bedroom curtains woke Callie up. Surprised Joe wasn't in the bed beside her, she sat up listening intently to the house's sounds. Everything was quiet except for the early morning calls of the Carolina wrens outside her window. *What is he up to this morning? He usually sleeps in on Saturday. Is that ham I smell? Oh, he's getting breakfast ready.*

Callie got up, pulled on some clothes, and went into the kitchen. "Hey, handsome. You plan on letting me sleep all day?" She stopped at the counter and fixed herself some coffee.

"No, but you seemed a little tired yesterday so I thought a little more rest would be good for the both of you." Joe turned from the stove to give her a kiss and gently pat her belly. "I'll cook some eggs when you're ready."

Callie wrinkled her nose as she went to the kitchen table and sat down. "My stomach feels a little off. But I'll try to eat."

Frowning slightly, Joe walked up beside her and began rubbing her shoulders. "Is it morning sickness?"

Callie grinned and shrugged her shoulders. “Probably. The doctor’s office said there wasn’t much they could do about it. Think I’ll just start with toast.” She started to get up, but Joe gently pressed down on her shoulders.

“You sit here. I’ll get your toast,” he said. He hurried across the kitchen and put two slices of bread in the toaster.

“Honey, you know I’m not sick or anything.” Callie smiled as she watched Joe take a bread and butter plate from the cabinet.

He looked over his shoulder and smiled back at her. “I know. And I know you’ll have to manage while I’m at work. But—right now I’m home.”

When it was ready, Joe brought Callie her toast and went to fix himself more coffee. “Thanks, sweetheart. I’m sure this will pass,” Callie said and began munching on the toast.

Joe came to the table and sat down beside her. “I’ll wait for a while before starting the eggs. Are you sure there’s nothing they can do about morning sickness?”

“Not really. Momma said eating a few saltines could help when I asked her about it yesterday.” Callie tilted her head to the side to look at Joe. “I think I can eat breakfast now. The queasiness is gone.”

“I’ll fix those eggs and warm the ham up.” Joe pushed his chair away from the table and went back to the stove. “So what do you want to do today?” After the pan was warm, he put four eggs in the large skillet.

“I think we should work on combining the guest room and my sewing room.” Callie got up to make more coffee. “Momma and Dad want to come down in a couple of weeks. I’d like to have that room ready for them.”

Joe tossed the empty eggshells into the trash. “All right, if you’re feeling up to it, we can start after we eat.”

With breakfast over, Callie collected the plates and silverware from the table. “I’ll just rinse these for now and then we can get started on the rooms.”

Working together, they had everything moved into the sewing room before lunch. Callie tossed the curtains from the guest room into the washing machine along with the bedspread. “Hey, we still have some ham. Do you want a sandwich?” she asked, going back to the sewing room where Joe was setting up the bed.

“That sounds good, honey. I’ll be there in a minute.” Joe lowered the box springs onto the bed before going into the hall to get the mattress.

“There’s some slaw left. Want some of that?” Callie stood out of the way in the hall.

Joe grunted as he picked up the mattress. “Sure.”

She chuckled. “I could help with that you know.”

“I’ve got it.” Joe plopped the mattress onto the bed. “I’ll just have to straighten it a little.”

“I’ll go make our lunch.” Callie walked back to the kitchen. By the time Joe sat down, their lunches were on the table along with two glasses of tea.

“So what’s after lunch?” Joe asked as he picked up his sandwich.

Swallowing her bite of slaw, Callie was thoughtful for a minute. “We just have to get the bed made and move my sewing table. I’ll iron the curtains tomorrow.”

“I thought we might go to the Isle of Palms for supper. They’ve got a nice seafood place there. It’s not fancy but it is a treat---to celebrate.”

“Ah, that’d be nice. We haven’t gone out in a while.” Callie set her fork on the table.

Joe reached out to hold her hand. “I know, we’ve been so focused on saving money. But before we eat, I’d like to go to Mount Pleasant.”

“Well, okay.” Callie looked at him quizzically. “What’s in Mount Pleasant?”

“I want to buy paint so I can paint the nursery tomorrow.” Joe paused and looked at the ceiling. “I want to look for a rocking chair.”

Callie chuckled. “I thought we weren’t going to buy stuff yet.”

Joe looked chagrined and shook his head. “It might take a while, but I want to find a rocking chair and refinish it for you and the little one.”

"Okay, honey. We can do that." Still chuckling softly to herself, she got up and cleared the table. "I'll just wash up these dishes and get the stuff into the dryer."

Joe found a parking place near the Mount Pleasant hardware store. The couple generally bought from small businesses. They liked the personal approach of most small business owners.

"Hi, Joe, Callie," Mike said as the bell on the door chimed. "What brings you to Mount Pleasant? Adding on to the house?"

"No, we're not getting that kind of addition," Joe said with a huge grin.

"Oh," Mike said looking at Callie and smiling. "So expecting a little one, are you?"

Callie blushed and smiled. "Yes, but not until September. We want to paint the nursery. Not sure what color I want though. But I know I don't want pink or blue."

Mike stepped out from behind the counter. "Come over here and look at these paint chips." The couple trailed behind him. "Do you know how you want to decorate the room? These days some people go for a Victorian look or even Mickey Mouse."

"I think we'll look a little." Callie started picking up different paint chips and putting them back into place. "Honey, I saw some really cute Winnie the Pooh fabrics when I was buying fabric for the porch slip-covers. What do you think about that?"

"That'd be cool. Whatever you want honey." Joe grimaced slightly. "Victorian's all lacy, isn't it? Not sure I'd like that."

"All that lace and frills just seems too hard to take care of." Callie wrinkled her nose. "What if we just paint the room a nice warm beige like this." Callie handed Joe a paint chip. "Then we can do whatever we want with the rest of the room."

"Are you sure that's what you want?" Joe looked from the chip to Callie's face.

"Yes, that's what I want." Callie turned to walk to the front of the store.

"That didn't take too long," Mike said when Joe handed him the paint chip. "That's a nice neutral color. Looks a little like sand. It'll take just a few minutes to mix it up. How many gallons do you need?"

"Two," Joe said. "I'll get some white for the baseboards. Callie, how about getting a couple of rollers and trim brushes."

With the paint and supplies taken care of they put their purchases in the back of the truck. "The used furniture place is in the next block. Do you feel like walking," Joe asked.

"Oh yeah, I'm supposed to keep doing stuff." Callie smiled up at him and linked her fingers with his before they started down the sidewalk.

Surprisingly, finding the rocking chair was a little harder. The chairs were either too small or too rustic for what Callie wanted. The salesperson suggested they try a store a couple of blocks over. The second store had the perfect rocking chair.

"Honey, this is the one," Callie said softly as she sank into the chair's wide seat, slipped off her shoes, and pulled her feet up to sit cross-legged. "It's big enough for reading bedtime stories when baby's older."

Joe took a few minutes to look over the rocking chair once Callie stood up. "Well, it's still very sturdy. And I know you love the white wicker." He reached over and squeezed her hand. "You'll probably want to sew covers for the cushions. But they're really not that worn."

Callie smiled softly while still holding his hand as she imagined rocking their baby to sleep. "That's really not hard. I can coordinate it with the curtains."

"Nice that the arms have that padded section. I can take it off so you can recover them. Wicker can get uncomfortable without it. Are you sure this is what you want?" He pulled Callie a little closer.

"It's like it was made for us and our baby." Callie stood on tiptoes to give him a
quick kiss. "Well then, let's get it paid for."

They made their way to the front of the store. Joe stopped for a moment. "You pay for this and I'll go get the truck."

Callie stood up and stretched while bracing her back with her hands. Beads of sweat dotted her forehead and she had to stop stretching to wipe them away. "Man, I'm glad there's only a couple more months to go." She took a moment to pull her hair back into a ponytail before settling onto the tall stool in front of the stove.

"You're bound to be uncomfortable," her mother said. "Glad I could come help you with the canning. It should go faster once the spaghetti sauce is done."

"I do appreciate it, Momma. I might be nuts for doing all this, but the garden was in already. Couldn't let it go to waste." Callie stirred the sauce. "I think this is ready to put in the jars." Placing the spoon on a saucer on the stove, she stood again.

"Okay, we'll just get it into the jars and then into the canner." Her mother lifted the large pot and placed it on several folded towels to protect the counter. "Can you set the jars next to me?"

"Here they are, Momma." Callie stepped back after placing the jars on the porcelain drainboard of the sink. "I wasn't sure about this drainboard at first, but it sure is handy for things like this."

"So easy to clean up, too." Her mother set the canning funnel in place and skillfully began to fill the jars. "Why don't you go lay down for a while? I can finish up here."

Callie hesitated. "I don't want to leave you with all the cleanup work."

"There's not much left." Giving her a sideways glance, her mother continued. "Besides, your baby shower is tonight, so you need to be rested for that. And Joe's parents will be here after supper."

Callie sighed as she leaned against the sink. "That's right we're supposed to be at Josie's at seven. Maybe I should take a rest. I won't be that long. Leave the cleanup for later. You don't want to over-tire yourself either."

"Just go take care of yourself and my grandbaby." Her mother paused to give Callie a hug. "I'll do whatever I can."

Looking down at her puffy ankles, Callie shook her head slowly. “Okay, Momma you win. I’ll go rest.”

Hmm? What is that I smell? Sure smells good. What time is it? Callie sat up on the bed and looked at the clock on her dresser. *Five o’clock? Joe’ll be home any minute.* She took another deep breath as she slipped into her shoes. *Aw, Momma’s gone and cooked supper.* She stopped long enough to run a brush through her hair and put it in a ponytail before hurrying into the kitchen.

“Momma, you didn’t have to do all this.” Callie frowned slightly. *I should be cooking after everything Momma’s done today.* “Did you even rest?”

Her mother turned from the stove to face her. “Yes, I did lay down for half an hour or so. Your dad caught some flounder so I thought we could have that for supper along with some slaw and hush puppies.” Despite her mother’s calm voice, her knuckles were white as they gripped the spoon.

Callie went to the cabinet to get a glass for iced tea while she figured out what else needed to be done to get supper ready. “Okay, I’ll make the slaw once I finish this tea.”

“Already done.” Her mother smiled. “I brought you a mandolin like mine, so it was easy to get that done.”

“All right, the hush puppies then.” Callie watched her mother’s smile turn into a grin. “Dad’s at Pete’s. We ordered enough hush puppies for everyone.” Briefly hiding her face with her hand, she continued. “You know I don’t make hush puppies.”

Speechless, Callie sank into a chair. “Momma. I could have done that.”

“I know you can, sweetie, but Dad and I wanted to do this for you. If we lived closer, I could just stop in and do a little something here and there. Let me do what I can while I’m here.”

Callie put her feet up on the chair next to her and was quiet for a minute. *Momma’s just helping. The least I can do is accept it with grace.* “Thank you, Momma. My feet and back do hurt.” Callie watched her mother's shoulders relax and knew she had made the right decision. "I'll just set the table in a few minutes. It shouldn't be long before Joe is home."

They had a pleasant family meal after Joe's arrival. He was appreciative of his mother-in-law's cooking. Joe's parents arrived shortly after dinner was over so his mother could go to the shower. His parents were staying in a motel in Mt. Pleasant.

There was just enough time to clean up and change before the baby shower. Since this was a women's only affair, Joe and the other men decided to check the shrimp pots they put out every day since Callie and her mother were canning today and didn't get to it.

The next morning everyone had breakfast before gathering in the nursery to look at the presents the couple received at the shower. Joe was sitting on a cushion at Callie's feet. Her parents perched on the toy chest and his parents sat in a couple chairs brought in from the kitchen.

"Sorry, I was asleep when you got back last night." Joe grinned sheepishly. "They were pushing us to finish the job so we could start a new one on Monday."

"It's all right honey." Callie smiled down at Joe from her rocking chair. "You don't usually work on Saturday and then to have to work the full day." Callie shook her head slowly.

"Nobody can call you a slacker," her dad said. "And I can see you're pretty attentive to my Callie-girl. Always have been." He reached over to lightly punch Joe on the shoulder.

"Well, thanks, Dad." Joe ducked his head for a moment before getting up from the floor. "Let me get a couple of chairs. You guys look cramped sitting on the toy chest. Even if it does have a cushion, you can't be too comfortable."

Joe returned with the chairs, and after people resettled, he picked up the seagrass basket Alma had given them. "So what will we do with this?" He asked, looking at the oval basket with two handles and then over at Callie.

"It's a little bassinet. The handles are pretty strong so I could move it around the house or put it in the car. Baskets like this last for generations. Alma is so kind and generous." Nearly overcome with tears of happiness, Callie sniffled and wiggled her nose.

"Callie, I really like the bunny theme. A bit like Beatrice Potter, but not too much." Joe's mother picked up a stack of muslin receiving blankets covered with tiny bunnies. Each bunny wore a short pinafore or jacket in muted primary colors. "Everything will come together nicely."

"I think it will. Glad you like the bunnies. The more I looked at Winnie the Pooh the more I felt like I was in a cartoon."

"Yeah, these bunnies are good for a boy or girl." Her dad stood up, walked over to the window and looked outside. "Nice light in this room."

"We got so many nice things. Thank you again, for the crib." Callie's eyes danced with excitement. "You got me there. Since you waited until we left to put it together, I was totally surprised. And Dad Stevens, this rocking horse is so precious. I love the little padded saddle and the mane."

"Well, Momma made the saddle and fashioned the mane and tail from a new mophead." The Stevens grinned over Callie's obvious appreciation of the gift.

In a few minutes, they had the presents neatly stacked in the crib. "Okay, we've got things sorted. I can wash them later. Let's go eat lunch."

Over lunch, the talk centered on preparations for the baby's arrival. "Now don't forget. I'll come down after baby's born and stay for a week." Her mother looked at Callie. "I know you're planning to breastfeed, but I can run the house so you can take care of the baby and rest."

"And I'll be down the week after that." Joe's mother nodded with determination.

"I'm sure I can manage." Callie looked at her mother intently.

"Not saying you couldn't. But you don't have to." Her mother smiled. "Your Aunt Sally and I did this for each other when our children were born. Let me tell you, you'll be more tired than you think possible."

Joe's mother smiled. "I've never been as tired as I was after Joe was born. I'm glad you're letting me help."

"Okay, okay." Callie looked at her hands folded in her lap. She wasn't sure how she felt about this offer. *Momma's trying to help. As long as she doesn't get too nervous about the baby. And I couldn't refuse her while letting Mom Stevens help.*

Joe grinned and winked at her when she looked up. Callie couldn't help but smile back. "Maybe, then I can get that furniture refinished."

Her dad picked up the change in topic. "You did a great job on the rocking chair. Now what's the hold up with the other furniture?"

"Seems Callie's allergic to the polyurethane. When I brought it inside, she broke out in a rash and then had trouble breathing." Joe shook his head and grimaced when he remembered how afraid he'd been on the way to the hospital. "Had to leave it on the porch for over two months for the fumes to die down."

Her dad frowned and cocked his eyebrow. "Really, Callie? I refinished furniture all your life."

"I don't know, dad. The doctor said it'd probably go away after the baby is born." Callie shrugged. "I hate that half the furniture doesn't match. Of course, Joe's had to work so much overtime lately." Her voice trailed off.

Her dad laughed and then got serious. "Callie-girl, I'm not finding fault." He reached over to pat her shoulder. "You guys have done a wonderful job with the nursery. Heck, with the whole house."

Her mother chimed in. "Better it's all in here and not where you can't use it. Now you can just put things away as you feel up to it."

Callie sighed. "Okay, I just didn't want you to think badly of Joe." She reached over to squeeze her husband's hand.

"You know better than that. Your mother and I both know he's been devoted to you since high school," her dad said, punching Joe on the shoulder again before he continued. "And he's not afraid to work hard or do anything else to prove it."

Joe blushed slightly and held up his hand to forestall any more conversation along that line. "Okay, enough now. How about you old hands take a look at these lower cabinets next to the sink with me? When we get ahead again after the baby's born, I'm thinking about putting in a dishwasher for her."

Callie cleared the table and stacked the dishes on the counter while the men knelt to look under the sink. "I'll get these few things later. If you've got everything packed for your trip home, let's go out to the front porch."

The three women sat on the porch enjoying the cool breeze. "Mom Stevens, I really appreciate the rocking horse and the cute outfits." Callie shifted in the porch swing. "Glad you could meet some of our friends. But I hate that you guys had to stay in a motel."

Joe's mom waved a hand and smiled. "Don't think anything of it. I'm just happy we could come."

They continued talking about babies until the men joined them on the porch. "I hate to break this up Callie-girl, but Momma and I really should be heading back." As she stood up, her dad hugged her. "Now you take care of yourself. We'll call when we get home."

"Thanks for everything." Joe picked up their suitcase as he and Callie followed her parents to the car. "Now I see how to get that dishwasher in place when the time comes."

When the couple walked back to the porch, Joe's parents were preparing to leave. Callie and Joe retraced their steps to the driveway as his parents went to their car. Callie hugged his mother. "Thanks again for coming."

"Wouldn't have missed it for the world," Joe's mother said holding her daughter in law tightly.

"Well, we should get going." Joe's dad tapped the hood of the car lightly.JoJo

"Okay, Dad." Joe laughed, walked over to Callie, and put an arm around her waist. "Let us know when you get home."

They cleaned the kitchen after supper. Then she and Joe sat in the loveseat on the front porch. "Honey, this is the life." Joe took a deep breath. "Smell that honeysuckle. And look, the herons are coming back in." He pointed to a pair of blue-gray birds in the sky moving toward the tidal basin hidden from their view by large live oak trees. "This is surely the best place to live." He turned to smile at Callie and linked his fingers with hers.

Callie groaned softly and lifted her legs onto the coffee table in front of them. "You're so right." She placed his hand across her belly and looked carefully at his face. "Feel that?" Her smile widened to a grin as she watched Joe's face light up when the baby delivered a strong kick.

"You know, I feel the baby move nearly every day now and each time it's just so amazing that you can grow a little one inside you." Joe kissed her gently and leaned toward her until their heads were touching. "Have you thought any more about names?"

"We narrowed the list down. I'd like Kimberly Mae if the baby's a girl and Joseph Robert if we have a boy." Callie squeezed his hand resting on her belly.

"Now remind me, I know Robert is for your dad. And is Mae your mother's middle name?" He looked at her quizzically.

"That's right. Are you still okay with those names? I figure we can get more of your family names in later." Callie bumped her head lightly against his.

"They're perfect," he murmured. "Look at that sunset. It's beautiful."

With its last rays, the sun painted the sky with shades of orange, rose, and purple. Callie and Joe watched without a sound as the purple crept in and darkness fell. The birds too fell silent as they settled down for the night. Only an occasional whippoorwill's mournful cry broke the evening's calm.

16

Caines Island 1969

Callie woke to darkness. *Is that Kimberly? Ugh. My chest is all wet.* She slipped out of bed careful not to wake Joe since he had to go to work in a few hours. Picking up the small towel from her nightstand, Callie dried herself and peered into the bassinet. *Ah, you're just beginning to wake up my little lovely. I'll grab my robe and then we'll go to your room.*

After slipping out of the damp gown and into her robe, Callie picked up her tiny daughter and cooed softly to her while she made her way to the nursery. She fumbled a little getting the diaper snug around Kimberly's waist. "Sorry that was such a process." Callie picked up her now squirming daughter whose face was getting red as she began to cry. "Momma's got you. Let me get settled in the rocking chair and then you can eat."

Joe crept into the room while Callie was putting Kimberly in the crib. He stopped behind her, peered over her shoulder, and gave her a gentle hug. "She's perfectly beautiful. Such a cute nose."

"She is absolutely perfect." Callie took his hand and led him from the room. "She needs to sleep for a while. I haven't heard Momma moving around yet."

"I started coffee. Are you going back to bed? You need to rest, too," Joe said as they walked hand in hand to the kitchen.

"Not right now. I'm sticky from leaking milk. I'll have to get a shower when you're done."

Joe kissed her nose gently. "No, you go ahead."

Letting go of his hand Callie went into the bathroom to shower. Returning to the kitchen, still in her robe, she poured a cup of coffee. "I guess I'll have to sleep in one of my nursing bras so I can use a pad to keep it from running all over me." Callie laughed as she brought the coffee to the table.

Joe smiled at her when she sat down with him. "Well, I guess it's good you're making a lot of milk?"

"Yeah, I think I can start freezing some of it soon. That would let you feed her without using the formula." Callie put her elbow on the table and rested her head on her hand. "What I'm really happy about," she said yawning, "is that the coffee doesn't seem to bother her. I'd be asleep on my feet without it."

Joe stood up, went to the sink, and rinsed out his cup. "I'll get my shower now. Don't worry about breakfast. I'll grab a sandwich at Pete's on my way out."

"Okay." Callie yawned again and went to their bedroom to get dressed. *I'm glad Momma's still sleeping. I'll just lie here a minute. I never knew I could be so tired.* She didn't wake when Joe gently covered her with the bedspread before he left for work.

Oh no, not again. Knew I should've gotten dressed. Callie woke up with milk dribbling down her chest. *Here we go again. Now my robe is wet. Let's see what I can put on to feed Kimberly. At least she's not crying.* After drying herself off, she slipped into one of her nursing nightgowns and hurried to the nursery. *This will work since no one's here, except Momma and me.*

She stopped at the nursery door, watching her mother as she cooed and smiled while gently rocking Kimberly. *They're so cute. I hate to break this up.* "Morning, Momma. I'm awake now."

Her mother looked up still smiling. "Joe told me you were sleeping before he left. Glad you were able to get some rest."

"I did. Never knew having a baby would be so exhausting," Callie said as she lifted the infant from her mother's arms and settled into the rocking chair after her mother stood up.

"I'll just go into the kitchen. I'm sure something needs doing in there." Her mother hesitated as she turned to leave.

"No, you don't have to go." Callie pointed to the armchair Joe had brought into the room last night. "That's why we brought the other chair in."

"Well, okay. I'll get some coffee for me and some water for you." Her mother returned in a few minutes. "Here's your water."

"Thanks, Momma. I keep forgetting to drink a glass of water while I'm nursing." Callie frowned pensively for a minute. "At her next feeding, you can give Kimberly some formula, if you want."

Her mother looked thoughtful. "Won't that mess with your milk production? Although, since I gave you and Bobby formula, I have to say I don't know much about breastfeeding."

"Oh, no. It'll be okay. The nurses told me to supplement with formula at first. I'm going to manually express some milk so I can freeze it." She shifted Kimberly to her other breast. "I'm lucky that my milk came in so well this early."

Her mother sat folding diapers while Kimberly finished eating. "She sure seems like a happy, healthy baby."

Callie looked down to see her daughter was drifting off to sleep. "She has a check-up on Friday. Can you stay long enough to take us?" Callie asked as she settled her daughter in the crib and turned to leave the room.

Her mother left a stack of diapers on the changing table and followed Callie out of the nursery. "That's no problem. Thought I'd stay until Saturday morning."

In the hall, Callie turned to hug her mother. "Thank you. It's been such a help having you here. I'm going to get another shower now before Kimberly wakes up."

Friday Callie's mother drove them to the appointment with Kimberly's pediatrician. The doctor told them Kimberly was doing well and that Callie could drop the formula feedings whenever she was ready.

As they were settling in the car afterward, her mother asked. "Do you feel like stopping in Peebles before we go home? I saw some sleep bras in their sale paper I think you'd like. Then you could stop sleeping in the nursing bras. That's got to be uncomfortable."

"If we don't take too long. It'll be good to do something different." Callie grinned at her mother.

In the store, they were able to find what they wanted quickly. Callie's mother found a few more nursing nightgowns that Callie liked. At the register, she and Callie argued briefly about paying for the items. "Momma, I can buy my own clothes." Callie insisted.

"I know you can. But this is something I want to do for you. Dad and I bought things for Kimberly, but I know it's nice to have something new when you're feeling so tired."

"All right, if you insist." Callie shook her head. *Momma's so stubborn sometimes.* Her mouth formed an O when her mother instructed the sales clerk to find three more bras in Callie's size.

"Not a word, Callie," her mother said wagging her finger at her daughter. "I insist. This way, you won't have to do laundry so often. Lord knows Kimberly creates enough of that."

Callie couldn't help but laugh thinking about the loads of diapers they had washed in the past week. "Okay, Momma. Thank you. I appreciate it."

Saturday morning while Callie and her mother cared for Kimberly, Joe started breakfast. Leaving the kitchen to check on them, he quietly walked into the nursery. Seeing his daughter asleep in Callie's arms, he whispered, "Bacon's ready. I'll make eggs when you come out to the kitchen."

Callie nodded as she got up to put Kimberly in her crib. For a moment, the three adults stood entranced while they stared down at the tiny baby. Callie waved her hand toward the door and the three of them tiptoed out.

In the kitchen, Callie poured coffee for everyone. "I can finish this if you want, Joe."

"Nah, I can fry up a couple of eggs. I got to sleep in this morning. You and Mom need to sit for a little while." Joe said after putting milk and sugar in his coffee.

"All right." Callie added milk to her coffee and joined her mother at the kitchen table. "Momma, have you got everything packed?"

"I think I've got everything. I did most of the packing last night after supper." Her mother took a few sips of her coffee. "I should have good weather for the drive home."

"The forecast sounded good this morning when I was listening to the news," Joe said as he put two over medium eggs and a slice of toast on a plate and took it to the table along with a platter of bacon. "Here you are, Mom. Callie, yours will be ready in a couple of minutes."

"Actually, honey. I only want one egg this morning." Callie went to the refrigerator. "Does anyone else want orange juice?"

Joe and her mother nodded so she poured three glasses of juice. She sat down as Joe put their plates on the table. The three of them finished breakfast and talked about the upcoming week.

"We don't have any appointments for a couple of weeks, and I'll be driving again by them. Joe's mom will be here to help starting tomorrow." Callie began clearing dishes from the table. "I'll just rinse these now and wash them after you leave, Momma."

Her mother pushed her chair back and stood up. "I'd better go ahead and get on the road. Or else I'll be here all day."

The small family was on the front porch enjoying the balmy evening when Joe's mother, Melinda, called. Joe's face crumpled when his mother told him about his father's heart attack. His dad would be home in a few days, but she needed to stay with him. "Of course, Momma. You need to be with Dad. We'll be fine here. I'll try to get to Columbia next weekend. I'm not sure when Callie will be up to traveling, but we'll all come when we can."

Sunday, Max, Louise, Joe, and Callie sat on the front porch sipping iced tea. "Callie, you're looking good," Louise said.

"Thanks, Louise. Max, how are things going on the pier?" Callie asked, turning to look at Max.

"It was slow starting, but things are picking up." Max took a drink of tea. "Sorry to hear about your father's heart attack, Joe. Are you guys going to Columbia?"

Joe frowned slightly. "I plan to go next weekend. I'm uneasy about leaving Callie here without the truck though."

Louise held her hand palm up in a stop motion. "Callie could call us if she needed anything. We're not going anywhere next weekend."

Joe pursed his lips thoughtfully. "What do you think, honey?" Joe looked at Callie.

"It'll be okay. You need to go. I wish I could go with you—" Callie stopped speaking when Joe frowned and shook his head.

'"She's not a month old. And you, you don't have your strength back. If you're okay about it, I'll leave Friday after work and come home Sunday." Joe looked at Callie intently.

"I'll be fine. Alma, Max, and Louise are just a phone call away." Callie jutted her chin out.

Joe sighed deeply knowing it would be useless to argue further. "Okay. I'll do it. I really would like to see how he's doing. Max, Louise, thank you so much."

Max flapped a hand at Joe. "Think nothing of it. You three have become part of the island family."

Friday night Joe quietly entered his parents' home using his key. Setting his suitcase down by the front door, he was surprised to see his mother waiting for him in her favorite armchair in the living room.

"Mom, I'm surprised you're still up," he said with a smile as he crossed the room and leaned over to give her a hug.

"I was a little worried with you traveling after work." Her hands fluttered down and she patted his arm before she released him from the embrace. "I know you're a careful driver, but you don't know about the other fools on the road." Although she smiled up at her son, the deep lines in her face and the circles under her eyes made the strain she was under obvious.

"How's Dad doing?" Joe moved toward the couch.

"Let's go in the kitchen. Are you hungry?" His mother stood up and turned to leave the room.

Joe reversed his direction and followed his mother. "No I ate a couple of sandwiches Callie made for me on the way up. I'll just get something to drink. You sit down. I can get it."

His mother sat at the kitchen table. She traced the patterns in the green Formica top. "Doctors all say he's doing as well as can be expected. Today he sat in the living room for a quite a while."

Joe frowned a moment and he sat beside his mother. "Well, that's a good thing, isn't it? He reached out to gently hold his mother's hand.

She nodded with tears in the corners of her eyes. "Yes. I'm just so worried for him. You know he had the heart attack at work. And when I first saw him at the hospital, he was so deathly pale." She paused, squeezing back her tears. "I don't know what I'll do if we lose him."

Joe leaned over and held his mother in his arms. With her head on his shoulder, she cried quietly as Joe rubbed small circles on her back. After a few minutes, she sniffled and moved away, sitting up taller in her chair. "Oh Joe. Sorry about that boohooing and pulling you away from your family."

He patted his mother's hand. "You have to cry sometime and I know you keep up a brave front around Dad. Don't worry about Callie and Kimberly. Our friends are looking out for them." Joe tried to hide a yawn behind his hand.

"Let's get to bed. You've got to be exhausted." His mother stood up and took Joe's glass to the sink. "We've been sleeping later since he got out of the hospital."

"We'll all sleep until we get up in the morning." Joe hugged his mother and got his suitcase from the living room before going to bed.

Saturday morning, Joe sat with his dad on the front porch trying not to make a face at the taste of decaf coffee. Apparently, it was one of the many dietary measures his dad had to adjust to. "I can't believe that a man with dairy cows is having to eat margarine." His dad shook his head in disgust.

Joe chuckled. "Maybe you'll get used to it. They say butter is bad for your cholesterol." He watched as his dad appeared to be nodding off. "Hey, Dad. Let's go inside. Maybe you could sit in the recliner. I'll hang out in the living room with you."

With a deep sigh that moved his shoulders up and down, his dad slowly stood up and made his way inside. "I just seem to fall asleep no matter what's going on. Doing anything makes me so tired."

"That's got to be frustrating." Joe sat on the couch as his dad settled in his recliner. "And if you fall asleep, I'll just read the paper if you."

"I think there's a baseball game tonight. I forget who the Braves are playing. Maybe we'll watch it later." It wasn't long before his dad was sleeping deeply.

Joe read the paper for a while and decided this would be a good time to mow the yard. Although the grass wasn't that high, he knew it would bother his dad that the grass had not been cut for two weeks. His dad always mowed once a week, on Wednesdays. With any luck this would be the last time the yard needed to be mowed this season. After cleaning and putting away the mower. Joe looked around the shed and seeing that nothing else needed to be done, he went back to the house. He came in through the kitchen door and went to the refrigerator. "Is Dad still asleep?"

His mother looked up from the cookbook in front of her and nodded.

After pouring himself a glass of tea, he joined her at the table. "What have you
got there, Momma."

"Just looking for a different way to bake chicken." She grimaced. "His doctors say he shouldn't eat fried foods."

"That's got to be hard learning to cook all over again." Joe thought a minute. "Callie sometimes bakes chicken in Italian dressing. Tastes pretty good."

His mother tilted her head. "He might like that. Of course, we're using a salt substitute that has some seasoning in it. Still when you're used to all the fat in your diet it's hard to change."

Joe nodded in agreement. "Maybe when Callie and Kimberly come up with me next time, we'll bring along some seafood. We've got a pretty good supply in the freezer since we fish at least once a week and Callie has shrimp pots in the water all the time so it really doesn't cost anything."

"That would make for a nice change. I remember Callie making a really good seafood boil and a gumbo. I'll have to ask her how she makes it."

"I'll get her to send the recipe to you." Joe stood up and pushed his chair under the table.

"Joe, are you there in the kitchen?" His dad called from the living room.

"Be right there, Dad." Joe put his glass in the sink and returned to the living room.

"Did I hear the mower going?" His dad frowned slightly. "Didn't mean for you to be doing stuff like that."

Joe smiled and shrugged. "Just thought I'd keep myself busy and help out while you were resting. I knew that having the grass that tall was making you crazy. Oh, yeah, what time are the cows used to being milked?" He asked as he settled himself on the couch again.

"Well, I do appreciate it. And don't worry about the cows. Jim's been taking care of them. We'll just keep things steady for him since I don't know when I'll be up to doing it myself." His dad turned in his chair to look at Joe. "Just feel so useless right now."

Joe tilted his head. "I can imagine, but you'll get back to your old self. It's just going to take some time. And if you want to have Jim take care of the cows, I understand." He gave his dad a light punch on the arm.

When his mother joined them in the living room, Joe launched into a description of Kimberly and talked about what a wonderful mother Callie was. He promised to send pictures when they got them back from the drug store where they took the film to be developed.

"So she's got red hair like Callie's mother," his mother said. "You know my momma had red hair. Not that you'd remember. By the time you came along it was all gray."

"No, I didn't. We were kinda surprised since our hair is dark." A smile spread across Joe's face. "That's really cool."

After a quiet supper, Joe and his parents watched the Braves game until everyone decided to call it a night. In the morning, they had a light breakfast of fruit, toast, and scrambled Eggbeaters. Joe still didn't think decaf was really coffee, but drank it anyway in solidarity with his dad.

"I've gotten used to this breakfast. Just miss your momma's wonderful gravy at supper," his dad said as he leaned back in his chair. "How about walk out to the barn with me before you go. I need to get some exercise in."

When they returned from their tour of the barn, his mother came out to the porch. Once his dad settled next to her in one of their matching rocking chairs, Joe loaded his suitcase in the truck and returned to the porch to hug his parents.

"Son, it's been great having you here," his dad said as Joe leaned over to give him a hug.

"I'm glad I could make it. Now you call if you need help with anything." Joe stood up and turned to hug his mother.

"Now, Momma, you remember to rest, too." Joe said leaning over to hug her.

"I'll see what I can do about that. Just call when you get home, so I know you made it safely." His mother patted his arms as he straightened.

"I will Momma." Not wanting his parents to see the tears in his eyes, Joe hurried to the truck.

Over the next few months, it was easy to see Joe doted on his daughter. At her slightest sound, he was at her side. Before she started sleeping through the night, many times he got up with her, often sending Callie back to bed. When they went on family walks, he frequently carried her in the sling and named all the birds for her, especially the sandpipers, telling her they were his favorites. In the evening, he'd dance through the house singing "My Cherie Amore" while holding her close to his chest while she stared up at him and cooed along with him.

November finally arrived and the little family prepared for the drive to Columbia for Thanksgiving. "Okay honey, I think I've got everything packed." Callie ran her fingers through her hair as she walked into the kitchen where Joe was dancing with Kimberly.

"Two suitcases?" Joe asked with a small frown. "We're just going for three days. And what's this other bag?"

"There's a suitcase for us and one for Kimberly. Then there's her diaper bag and the seagrass bassinet for naps at your parents' house. Oh and don't forget the cooler for your parents. You know, we'll have to stop and change her on the way." Callie pulled her long dark hair into a ponytail.

Joe grinned and shrugged. "I forget how much stuff she needs. Okay, I'll load this up." He gave Callie a quick kiss and handed her their smiling daughter.

Halfway to Columbia, the truck's engine began overheating. "I've got to pull over and check this out." Joe closed his eyes and rubbed his forehead.

"I'll see if Kimberly wants to eat while we're here. At least, I'll get her diaper changed." Callie puffed out a breath and slid out of the truck with Kimberly in her arms. Laying the baby on the seat, she quickly changed her diaper. She was back in the truck with the baby at her breast when Joe climbed in beside her.

"We're going to have to replace the truck before long. I can get us to Columbia and back, but---" His shoulders sagged and a worried frown creased his forehead. "I was hoping to keep this thing going and pick up a car for you."

"I don't need a car. You've got to get to work." Callie squeezed his shoulder. "If I need anything in town, we can go on the weekend."

"Every day it seems like something else is wrong with this poor old thing." Joe paused a moment and chuckled. "Heck, I got this truck when I was in high school and it was old then."

Callie grinned and nodded. "It's been a good truck. We'll just have to save some and be on the lookout for a good deal. It's going to be okay."

They made it to Columbia without further problems with the truck. The whole family, including Bobby and Susan, who had arrived from Charleston the day before, came out to help them carry their bags inside.

"Callie, it's so good to see you," Susan said as she hugged Callie and lifted the edge of the blanket to peek at Kimberly. "She's beautiful and man, what curly red hair."

"You want to hold her while I run to the bathroom?" Callie asked as she allowed Susan to take Kimberly into her arms. Giving her parents a quick hug, Callie darted inside.

Everyone had gathered in her mother's bright yellow kitchen when Callie returned to the group. Her mother now held Kimberly, cooing while the bright-eyed infant waved her arms and reached for her grandmother's fingers. "She's so alert, Callie," her mother said as she looked up briefly.

Callie looked at Joe and beamed before going to the coffee pot. "Guess we're doing all right then." She sat next to Susan at the table. "What's the plan for dinner tomorrow?"

"We'll eat around three. I think Joe Sr. and Melinda will be here around twelve." Her mother handed Kimberly to Joe. "I think she's ready to go to sleep. Does she need to eat?"

"She's not acting hungry. I'll just change her and lay her down in the bedroom." He paused by Callie's chair and kissed her on top of her head. "I've got this. You visit with your family."

Talk turned to Bobby and Susan. They were expecting their first child this summer. Both were ecstatic to be starting their family. "You know twins run in Susan's family," Bobby said glancing at his wife.

"It's way too early to tell but my grandma was a twin." Susan looked at Callie. "Are you managing to get some sleep? I hear it takes some babies a while to sleep through the night."

"She nurses around eleven and then doesn't wake up until around four thirty in the morning. So I'm doing okay in the sleep department." Callie tilted her head toward Susan and squeezed her hand. "It took me a little bit, but I finally learned to nap during at least one of her sleep periods during the day."

Susan nodded. "That's what my momma says, too. But I don't know how I'll ever get anything done if I do that."

"To be honest, having Momma come for a week was a life saver and then Joe helps with whatever needs to be done." Callie tilted her head toward her brother. "Something tells me, Bobby will be the same way."

Getting the Thanksgiving meal ready was a family affair even though Callie's mother had obviously been baking for days. Joe's parents arrived a little before noon. His dad looked gaunt and pale. When Callie expressed her concern, her father-in-law shared that under his doctor's instructions, he had lost nearly fifty pounds, but was still having bouts of angina. He refused to discuss his health further.

After dinner, Joe and the two older men went out to look at the truck and decided that tomorrow, when the stores were open, they could replace the radiator, hoping to keep the old truck running for a bit longer. All three men agreed the best thing would be to buy a new truck or at least replace the engine.

"Even a new engine will have to wait. We still owe a little on the hospital bill," Joe said, wiping his hands on a shop rag.

"Once you get your parts, bring the truck over and you can work in the barn. It'll keep you out of the wind." His dad slipped his ballcap off and ran a shaking hand over his thinning hair. "Are you sure you know how to do this, Joe?"

"I think so, Dad." Joe tugged at his ball cap. "I'll take a look at the auto parts store's Chilton's while I'm there."

His breathing a little ragged, Joe's dad leaned heavily on the truck's fender. "Bob, can you come with him tomorrow? I get tired out pretty easily these days. Keeping the radiator in place until you connect the hoses could be a hassle."

Bob knew Joe, Sr. was much like himself with a strong sense of family and knew that it took a lot for him to admit he couldn't help his son. "Sure, I'll bring Callie and the baby. That way you guys can visit without so much hullabaloo going on."

Once Joe and Bob repaired the truck, the young family split their time between each set of parents. Usually going over after breakfast and returning to Callie's parents before supper. It made sure Joe's parents had time with Kimberly without adding more work for his mom. Joe's dad was enthralled with Kimberly, holding her at every opportunity.

Saturday, Callie and Joe's mother sat at the kitchen table while Kimberly and Joe's dad were napping.

"Kimberly is such a healthy baby," she said, her hands fluttering up to her face and then down to the table. Even then she couldn't keep her fingers still and they tapped lightly against her coffee cup.

"Can I do something to help out while we're here?" Callie asked. "Maybe I could fix supper tonight. Looking after Dad Stevens has got to be wearing you out."

"No. Your mother's already got your supper planned, I'm sure. Oh, thanks for the recipes and all that seafood."

Callie waved a hand in dismissal. "You're welcome but it was really nothing. We always have the pots out and Joe's become quite the fisherman."

"Dad's just having a hard time coming to grips with this early retirement and having to hire more hands to help with the farm." Melinda's fingers continued to tap on her coffee cup.

"That's got to be really hard. I know he always planned to work the farm himself." Callie looked down at her hands. "Please let us know what we can do to help."

"Your being here with Kimberly is enough. It can't have been easy traveling in that truck with a baby." Joe's mother's hand fluttered over to give Callie's hand a squeeze. A small cry broke through the quiet house. Callie rose from her seat. "Let me go get her before she wakes up Dad Stevens."

Sunday Joe loaded up the truck after breakfast. The plan was to stop by his parents and leave after a short visit with them. The young family made it back to Caines Island without further trouble with the truck. Carrying Kimberly into the house, Callie breathed a sigh of relief. *It was great seeing everyone, but I'm sure glad to be home. Nothing smells as good as the salty air from the ocean.*

17

Caines Island 1970

Callie sat staring at the forlorn Christmas tree near the front window and the ring of dry, brown needles sprinkled over the tree skirt. The gray early morning light made the tableau all the more dreary. *I really didn't keep up with the tree this year. I almost forgot that we had Christmas. I've got to get the tree down today.*

With that thought in mind, she went into the closet in her sewing room to retrieve the boxes for ornaments. Peeking into the nursery, she saw Kimberly was still sleeping. Although she lingered a bit over the rocking horse shaped ornament labeled, "Baby's First Christmas", Callie managed to get the decorations off the tree and the tree onto the porch before Kimberly woke up for breakfast. Hearing her daughter's cries, she went to the nursery, gathered her daughter up close over her heart, and began to sing, "Hush little baby don't you cry..."

Later while Kimberly slept peacefully in the seagrass basket near her feet, Callie sat in one of the wicker rocking chairs on the front porch. Her gentle rocking mocked her frantic thoughts as she considered ways to earn enough money to stay on the island. *Too bad the insurance company wrote Joe's truck off as a total loss. The two hundred dollars the insurance company paid out went to pay utilities and the collection his coworkers had taken up will cover the next month's bills. But property taxes will be due soon. How am I going to do this? I know eventually I'll get a widows with-minors check from Social Security. It will help but I don't want us living hand to mouth either. I don't want to leave Kimberly with someone else even if I could find work off the island. Besides how would I get there?*

She carefully carried the seagrass basket with the still-sleeping infant inside and settled it in the patch of sunshine coming through the front window. Unable to quiet her thoughts she found an old composition notebook. *Maybe if I can organize my thoughts into lists it'll help me decide what to do.* After making a list of her expenses and what little money she had, Callie began going through her cabinets. *I've got enough canned goods and frozen food left from last year to last a few months. Okay, I've got a little time to figure this out.*

Kimberly began babbling in her basket. Callie smiled as she went into the living room and saw her daughter's tiny hands playing with the dust motes dancing in the sunlight. "Hello again my beautiful one. Did you have a good rest? Let's get you changed and then we can go for a walk. Momma's tired of being cooped up with her thoughts."

With her daughter changed and fed, Callie took Kimberly to her room and placed her in the middle of her double bed. "Now don't go figuring out how to roll over while I get changed." After pulling a loose dress over her head, Callie sat on the side of the bed and wrapped her dark braid around her head. Slipping on her Keds, Callie turned her attention to settling Kimberly into the sling that held the infant close to her chest. "Baby girl, these slings must be among the world's greatest inventions.

Walking slowly down the crushed oyster shell covered road to the beach, Callie forced all active thoughts out of her mind while she took in deep breaths of the salty air. The herons looked up from the tidal pools, but resumed their feeding as she passed. Seagulls squawked while they soared overhead. Crossing the dunes, Callie smiled as she caught sight of the sandpipers dancing with the foaming water while it lazily marked the shifting tides.

After a short while, she turned back and decided to walk along the pier and say hello to Max. He, along with others, sold a variety of things on the pier. During the summer, most people sold daily.

"Hey, Max. How's it going today?" Max sat cross-legged on the blanket where he displayed the hats and t-shirts he sold.

"I've had a real good day." Max grinned and pushed his hat back on his head.

Callie looked up and down the pier and a small thoughtful frown creased her forehead. "Does anyone sell fresh seafood? I don't think I've seen that."

"Well, no. Can't say anyone's doing that." Max looked at Callie a little more closely. "What are you thinking about?" He patted the blanket next to him, encouraging her to sit down.

"You know I have the shrimp and crab pots that I put out most days." She lifted the sling's flap so Kimberly would get the benefits of the sea breeze after she sat down. ' If I got a couple more pots and a large umbrella, Kimberly and I could sell seafood down here." Callie's frown eased While she considered the idea. "Heck, I walk further down the beach every day. Walking to the pier isn't as far."

"I think you're on to something there. Of course, you'd have to be careful about spoilage." Max paused while he helped a customer choose a hat. "But you really couldn't carry that much since you'll have Kimberly with you."

Callie nodded. "You're right there. It would be better to run out than have too much and it go bad. Does anyone need to know I'm selling on the pier?

"Nah, Pete keeps a sign up in the store. You might see if he'll add seafood to the list of things available on the pier." Max took off his hat and rubbed his hand across his close-cropped head. "You're right about that big umbrella since you've got Kimberly there."

Callie wiped the sweat from her brow as she looked earnestly at Max. "This seems like that could be the ticket for me. I really want to stay on the island."

On the way home Callie continued to think about her conversation with Max. The possibilities seemed boundless. *I'll be able to pay the bills and make a better life for me and Kimberly. We'll be able to stay on the island. In this house Joe and I fixed up together. I'll show Momma I know what is best for me and my daughter.*

Riptides: Book 2 of The Caines Island Stories

(Anticipated publication 2025)

Chapter 1 Callie April 1997

Her wicker rocking chair moved slowly in the ancient, comforting rhythm known to all who enjoy sitting in such chairs. Callie sipped her morning coffee. Every now and then it added a small creak to the sounds of the herons taking wing. She inhaled deeply, relishing the scent of magnolias in the light breeze, and then let her breath out slowly. Although the majestic old magnolia was but a shadow of its former self with its major leads gone, the arborist had done a good job salvaging it after hurricane Henry in eighty-seven. She and Luke had planted two more magnolias, several live oaks, and a few redbud trees and dogwoods once they completed renovations for the house.

Callie watched Kim's car drive away until the dense foliage along the roadside blocked her view. As the car disappeared, her thoughts went back to 1993. After getting her masters' degree and landing her first job, Kim had brought home her new boyfriend, Jake. Her daughter's face was aglow with newfound love.

"Hi, Momma, Luke." Kim called as the couple climbed out of the car. A huge grin spread across her face as she saw her mother and Luke waiting on the porch.

She hurried down the steps to hug her daughter. "Hey, sweetheart," she said as she held her daughter close. "Come on inside and get out of this heat."

Callie turned to give Jake a hug, but he had already gone to the back of the car to get their suitcase from the trunk. Hiding her disappointment, she slipped her arm around Kim's waist as the two women headed up the walkway. Once everybody was on the porch, Luke gave Kim a big hug and managed to get Jake to shake hands.

Jake remained taciturn during the visit. He did open up enough to let them know his family had moved to Charleston from New York when he was six. Even though he was a Registered Nurse and worked in the emergency room at one of Charleston's larger hospitals, Jake did not seem to share Kim's passion for the nursing profession. Kim laughed it off as his being jaded after seeing so many tragedies in the emergency room.

Shaking her head, Callie brought herself back to the present. Luke was already in his studio. *Something feels off. It shouldn't. Over the last ten years, we've all been able to rebuild our homes and the Emporium. Business is good. Kim and Jake married three years ago. Granted, I don't feel close to him, but I guess I can't expect everyone to look at family like I do. Besides, I've always encouraged Kim to handle things in her own way.* Callie continued her mental check-in on those she loved.

Alma seems a bit slower since her sister, Carol died, but she still comes into the store two or three times a week. Carol was the last of Alma's generation and her children are the only family Alma has now. It must be hard to realize that your family has scattered and those you love are already dead or dying.

Max and Louise are well. So's Momma and Dad. Same goes for Bobby and his family. Luke's family is doing well. Hell, he and I are better than ever. It's the spring of 1997 and life is good. So, what's wrong with me? Guess I'll figure it out; I usually do. Well, I'm due at the Emporium at ten this morning. Better get moving. Coffee cup in hand, Callie went inside.

She took a quick shower and towel dried her hair. It fell into a dark curtain just below her shoulders as she brushed it out before pulling it into a loose bun. *Still no gray. Guess that's the advantage of not having Momma's auburn coloring*. After pulling on loose slacks with a sleeveless top and over blouse, Callie slipped on her Keds before going to the kitchen to eat a bagel and have one more cup of coffee. Sitting at the kitchen island, as she pulled out her planner, she heard the back door open.

"Morning, love," Luke said as he walked up beside her and gave her a hug before getting his own coffee. Even though there was a coffee maker in the studio, he often took a break to join Callie before she started her day.

"Morning," Callie murmured.

"Do we have anything going on this week?" After grabbing a cup of coffee, Luke pulled out a chair and sat next to her. In the end, they decided to add the kitchen island since after the hurricane in eighty-seven Aunt Sally's vintage table wasn't salvageable.

Callie looked at her planner. "No. Jake is off this weekend so Kim will be staying in Charleston. And my family's not coming to the island until May."

"That's good. My parents have asked us to dinner on Friday. Not sure what time, but knowing them, it will be six-thirty or seven. Is that okay?" Luke rested his arm on the back of Callie's chair and gave her a light squeeze before turning his attention to his coffee.

"Yeah, that's fine. I should be out of the Emporium by five. It's still early spring so we haven't adjusted the hours." After making an entry for Friday's dinner, Callie slipped the planner back into her bag and stood up. "Give me a hug and kiss. I need to get going." Stepping back from Luke, she began to pick up her dishes.

"I'll get those into get the dishwasher before I go back to the studio. Later I'll talk to my mom and see what time dinner is," Luke said.

"Thanks, love," Callie said as she gave him a quick peck on the cheek before heading out the door.

Parking in front of the Emporium, Callie felt proud of what she, Max and Alma had accomplished. After hurricane Henry in eighty-seven, they replaced one of the large storefront windows and now it was a proper display window---more like a small, narrow room. They had covered the exterior concrete block with white stucco. A black and white striped awning stretched across the building. White wicker chairs with cushions to match the awning and a few small tables sat along the wide walkway in front of the store. To the left of the storefront window was a glass door which opened directly into the store's portion of the building. Further down and to the right of the large window was a set of double doors leading directly into the gallery. *We've really come a long way since our days of selling on the pier*. Callie smiled to herself

As she walked through the door, Max stuck his head out from their glassed-in office and waved for her to join him. Making her way to him, Callie greeted Shelia, one of the artists working in the store today. "How's it going?"

"Pretty good," Shelia answered. "Michael brought in a few new pieces so I'm shifting things around to be ready once you've checked them in."

"I'll do that in once I see what Max needs," Callie said over her shoulder as she continued on her way.

"Morning, Max. What's going on?" Callie asked as she put her bag down and joined him at the worktable. They still did all their planning and the Emporium's paperwork at a long table, although they did upgrade to comfortable office chairs and an actual rolling lateral file cabinet.

"Hey, Callie," Max said as he looked up from the ledger and smiled. "Nothing big. Louise and I are thinking about going on vacation, maybe take a cruise."

"Really? That's great. When are you going?"

Max shrugged and grinned. "I'm not sure. Louise is checking everything out. I just wanted to give you a heads up that I'd be out for a while this summer."

"I hope you can book one that gives you a few days in the Bahama's. Luke and I really enjoyed our honeymoon there. What brought this on?" Callie looked down at her lap. She had grown even closer to her partners as the years went by and had difficulty with the idea they would eventually retire or possibly develop some terrible ailment.

"I asked her what she wanted for her anniversary this year. You know we've been married for fifty-three years, and Louise likes to wear a bit of jewelry." Max paused and smiled. " And as the business grew, I was able to give her nicer stuff. But this year, I kinda wanted to do something special for her. She surprised me with this cruise idea."

"That sounds great, Max. Luke and I don't have any big summer plans so whenever you want to go is fine with me." Callie was happy for her friends and relieved there was no bad news. "You've both worked so hard all your lives. You deserve some fun. Is that Ethel I hear in the store?"

Callie turned in her chair so she could see out of the large window between the store and the office. "It is. Haven't seen her in a while. I'll see what she needs."

"Alright, I'll finish up here before heading home," Max said turning back to the ledger.

Callie watched as Ethel made her way through the store with a walker. Even with a walker, Ethel stood as straight and nearly as tall as the day Callie first met her. *Wow, Ethel's has really aged since Jack died. She must be at least ninety. Can't believe she's still here on the island, living alone in that house.* Callie smiled as Ethel approached the seafood counter. "Hi Ethel, what can I get for you today?" Callie said as she washed her hands and slipped on a pair of vinyl gloves.

"Well, you know me. I'd like three pounds of flounder," Ethel said with a grin. "The kids are coming to help me go through some stuff at the house for a yard sale."

Callie frowned slightly and then smiled. "You're going to do that and fry flounder? Ethel, you're amazing."

"Well, Stacy thinks she can do it if I sit in the kitchen with her. We're getting the place ready to sell. Probably should've moved after the hurricane in eighty-seven, but Jack had his heart set on staying on the island." Ethel turned her walker around so she could sit in it while Callie weighed and wrapped the flounder. " Anyway, the place is a lot for me to keep up with. The kids try to help, but they're so busy. It's not right for them to spend all their vacation time working down here," Ethel said. "And besides I don't like driving off the island and that makes shopping hard sometimes."

"Will you go to Fort Mill with Stacy?" Callie asked as she slipped the flounder into a bag.

"Yep. When they built the new house, they put in two master suites downstairs. It's big enough for me to have a small sitting area and I'll have my own bathroom with a walk in shower. It's real nice; I stay in it when I go to visit."

"Next time I go to the mainland, I'll give you a call to see if you want to come along," Callie said as she rang up the purchase. "That'll be five-fifty."

"Here you go." Ethel stood to hand Callie the money. "I might take you up on that offer of a ride into town." Ethel smiled as she placed her bag on the walker's seat.

"Get Stacy to call me, maybe I can help out. Getting a place ready for sale is a big job." Callie stepped around the counter.

"I'll do that. Though I expect she'll just come in with her own plan and that's okay. It makes my head hurt thinking about what I can take and what has to go." Ethel smiled and made her way through the store. She paused to wave at Shelia and Callie as she opened the door.

Callie wiped down the seafood counter and returned to the workroom to get Michael's new pieces into the inventory. With any luck she and Shelia would get them out in the gallery before closing.

"So how's Kim doing?" Max closed the ledger and began preparing to leave.

"She seemed quiet this trip and more tired than usual. Several times I thought she wanted to tell me something, but she only talked about the clinic and how much she likes working there." Callie put down her pen and looked at Max.

Max was thoughtful for a moment. "Did Jake come with her?"

"No. Apparently, he forgot they were coming this weekend and signed up for extra shifts at the hospital." Callie shook her head as she thought about how little she knew her son-in-law.

"I'm sure she'll tell you before long. You guys have always been close," Max said as he put away the ledger. "Alma's in tomorrow, right?"

Callie turned to look at the large wall calendar where they tracked days when they each would be in the store. "Yeah, she'll be here about noon. We don't have an artist in tomorrow. So I'll overlap with her. I should be here about eleven."

"That's good. We all need to look at those applications for a new delivery driver. Lewis has decided to enlist and working his notice, don't forget," Max said as he paused in the office doorway.

"Oh, that's right. I sure miss Danny, although I do see him at Alma's from time to time. He was so conscientious," Callie said. "You get on home. I need to get these things tagged so I can get them displayed this afternoon. See you tomorrow."

Here's a sample of *Against the Tide: Book 1 of the Caines Island Stories*.

1 Late Spring 1970

The ocean glittered with shimmering shades of pink, gold, and blue, reflecting the sun's rays as it worked its way above the horizon. The only sound is the squawking of seagulls as they soar and dip along in the wake of small fishing boats heading out to sea. Callie eased her baskets to the ground. *Not too much further.* She sat down and leaned against a live oak tree dripping with Spanish moss. Resting her baby in the V made by her legs and belly eased the strain on her back. She looked down, lifted the sling's flap, and smiled at her sleeping daughter. After a few minutes, she got up slowly to avoid jostling Kimberly, gathered her things and continues down the crushed oyster shell path. Before long, she was at the pier.

Callie set out her wares: shrimp, crab and a few seagrass baskets woven by her neighbor, Alma. The baskets are in demand and always sold out. Callie tried to keep things simple by bringing just enough to sell each day. *Kimberly will be a year old in a few months, and she's getting heavier by the minute. I'm going to have to find a cart or something soon. But first, I've got to figure out a way to stay on the island.*

Her mother wanted her to sell the house and move in with them. When Kimberly went to school, she could go to work in the mill. At least, those were her mom's thoughts on the matter. Her dad stood on the sidelines of this debate, knowing Callie would make up her own mind. Every visit or phone call from her mom involved some idea of rearranging their home to accommodate the two of them. Just last night, her mother was making the pitch again. Callie replayed the conversation in her head.

"Well, honey, you know we've left your room set up. The den could be Kimberly's nursery and playroom." Her mother's voice had the extra sweetness she added when trying to convince Callie to do something she didn't want to do.

"Momma, that's sweet, but where would Dad watch sports? You know he's got the Braves in the summer and then there's the Gamecocks during basketball season. And don't forget football."

"We can put the TV in the living room." Her mother countered.

"You don't care about any sport but baseball. What are you going to do when it's football season?" Callie laughed at her mental picture of her mother's impatience as her dad became excited and coached his favorite players from the comfort of his recliner.

"We'll get through that easy enough. We want to help you while you get on your feet. I didn't have to work while you and your brother were little. I don't want you to have to, either."

"Thanks Momma. But I really want to hold on to the house where Kimberly was born. Joe and I fixed it up together. Besides, it was Aunt Sally's. It needs to stay in the family. I've already made enough to pay the property taxes next week."

"But what about other expenses? And Kimberly's getting older. She's going to need even more of your attention. How are you going to do both?"

"I know it'll be hard. Raising Kimberly without Joe will be hard, no matter what I do. At least this way she will be with me. The social security check will start up soon and that will help. I'll figure out a way to make more money." Callie closed her eyes, hoping her mother wouldn't pick up on her frustration through the telephone.

"Your Dad and I are just trying to make things easier for you."

"I know, Momma, and I don't mean to seem ungrateful. I've got to try my idea first."

People strolling in from the boardwalk onto the pier broke into Callie's thoughts. Most chatted with vendors as they considered the wares for sale. Seemingly, many people enjoyed seeing what was available almost as much as they interested in finding a bargain. Others were there with a little more intent.

"Hi, Callie. Glad you've still got some shrimp. The kids are coming, and I was wanting some shrimp to go along with our oyster bake this evening."

"Good to see you, Ethel. All the family well?"

"You know Jack's back troubles him from time to time, but he's okay. Jill and her family are doing good. I hate they moved up to Fort Mill, but I guess you got to go where the work is. It'll be good to see them."

That was the last of her seafood. *Another good day.* Callie thought to herself. Kimberly woke up as Ethel headed down the pier. Callie adjusted the sling and put Kimberly to her breast as she sat crossed legged on the pier in the shade of her umbrella. Her long, dark brown hair and a lightweight muslin blanket screened the baby from the sun.

Alma's baskets always took a while longer to sell. She wove beautiful baskets but didn't use patterns favored by the Gullah artisans. "I learned basket weaving from them, but I won't cash in on their heritage. My people made baskets, too, but I paid little attention when I was younger," she once told her. A descendent of the Kiawah tribe, Alma was proud of her heritage. Her ancestors were farming and fishing here when the first white settlers arrived on the island. *Okay. With what I saved; I've made enough today to pay the light bill. Next in line is the phone bill.* Callie thought with relief.

Further down the pier, Callie noticed Max had set up a stand instead of spreading things out on the pier like most other vendors. He was selling straw hats and shirts. Callie thought to herself, *It would be more convenient to work from a stand. I wouldn't have to carry everything back and forth each day. I would make so much more money if I brought vegetables from my garden to the market, too.* After the last basket sold, she gathered her things and made her way over to Max.

"Hey, Max. How's business?" Callie sifted Kim's weight to ease the pull on her back.

"Was going pretty fast there for a bit. How 'bout you?" Max was a tall, ebony skinned man with flecks of gray in his hair. A fisherman in his younger days, Max had been selling shirts and hats since the rigors of fishing became too much for his aging body. Besides, his son didn't want to follow in the family fishing business. Steve was going to be a lawyer.

"My seafood sold out early. Had to wait a bit longer to sell all Alma's baskets. How did you wind up getting this stand?"

"Well, Steve told me the town supervisors wanted to encourage more sellers and tourists here at the pier. I set this up after getting a license for it. It's been good so far. If you're going to keep selling here, look into it."

"I just might do that. See you later. Gotta get Kimberly home now."

On her way home, Callie's mind reeled as she thought about building a stand of her own. *I could offer more things, like produce from her garden and loose sundresses for the tourists. Except for the license, I wouldn't need to put out more money. Lord knows I don't have any extra money. Not sure how Momma will take this. I know she didn't go back to work until Bobby and I were in school, but I don't see that I have much choice. Besides, it's 1970 and things are changing.*

Even with these thoughts swirling through her mind, Callie felt a surge of pride as she walked past her house to Alma's and looked at her home from the roadside. A modest white Cape Cod, with screened porches wrapping around three sides. Domer windows added character, although they only gave light to the attic. A neat, fenced yard surrounded the house. Small peach trees grew to the right of the driveway and should bear fruit this year. Late azaleas bloomed under the magnolia and live oak trees. Flower beds filled with zinnias, yarrow and rose campion followed the porches. Spanish moss streamed from most trees. Callie smiled to herself, thinking, *Joe and I did well.*

Alma waved from her front porch as Callie turned into the walk. "How'd we do today?" Alma was several years older than Callie. Even now, after years of working in vegetable fields, Alma stood tall and was fiercely independent. Her coppery skin and straight black hair belied her age. It had taken Callie a while to talk Alma into letting her take the baskets to the pier. Eventually, Alma understood it was Callie's way of repaying her for all the eggs and other things Alma saw as "just being neighborly" that she did for Callie.

"Sold out again. Here's your money from the baskets." Callie reached into her pocket with a smile.

"Come on in and have some iced tea. Let Kimberly loose on the floor." Alma turned to the front door. "Have a seat while I get the tea."

Immediately, as she stepped inside, Callie felt the cool air from the whirling ceiling fan and felt relieved. "That sounds great," Callie said as put her daughter on the living room floor and sat in one of Alma's comfortable armchairs. She loved the combination of the white shiplap walls and the bright oranges, reds and browns of the large rugs Alma had placed around the room. Their colors often seemed to reflect upward, reducing the starkness of the white walls covered with paintings and photographs. A large stone fireplace held center stage. Alma had filled it's mantel with more framed photographs.

"I'll be right out," Alma called from the kitchen.

Over the cool drinks, Callie told Alma about Max's stand and how she wanted to set up a stand herself.

"Sugar, that might be good. You'd need more stuff to sell, though."

"You're right. But I can sew the dresses myself. I've got a fairly good fabric stash to start with. I'd have to save more to buy the license and building materials." Callie bubbled with enthusiasm.

"Who's going to build it?" Alma sat her glass on a coaster out of Kimberly's reach.

Callie thought for a minute. “Me. Joe taught me some stuff when we were working on the house. I’ve still got his tools in the shed. I’m sure Dad will help me work out the plans.”

Alma’s dark eyes looked nearly black in the house’s cool shadows as she frowned in thought. “See how much it costs. We might be partners. I got a little put back from the baskets you’ve been selling for me.”

“I’ll see about it and let you know. Let me take this glass to the kitchen. I’d better get Kimberly home and cook something for supper.”

Printed in the USA
CPSIA information can be obtained
at www.ICGtesting.com
JSHW010423190824
68266JS00001B/18